VILLAIN SCHOOL
Hero in Disguise

VILLAIN SCHOOL
Hero in Disguise

Stephanie S. Sanders

BLOOMSBURY

NEW YORK   LONDON   NEW DELHI   SYDNEY

First published in the United States of America in October 2012
by Bloomsbury Books for Young Readers
www.bloomsburykids.com

For information about permission to reproduce selections from this book, write to
Permissions, Bloomsbury BFYR, 175 Fifth Avenue, New York, New York 10010

Library of Congress Cataloging-in-Publication Data
Sanders, Stephanie (Stephanie Summer).
Villain school : hero in disguise / by Stephanie S. Sanders. — 1st U.S. ed.
p.   cm.
Summary: When two new students arrive at Villain School, Rune Drexler discovers that
one of them is a hero in disguise and Rune, Countess Jezebel Dracula, and Big Bad Wolf
Junior must protect their school from the heroes.
ISBN 978-1-59990-907-3 (hardcover)
[1. Good and evil—Fiction.   2. Superheroes—Fiction.   3. Schools—Fiction.
4. Best friends—Fiction.   5. Friendship—Fiction.   6. Characters in literature—Fiction.]
I. Title.   II. Title: Hero in disguise.
PZ7.S1978832Vj 2012   [Fic]—dc23   2011051124

Book design by Donna Mark
Typeset by Westchester Book Composition
Printed in the U.S.A. by Quad/Graphics, Fairfield, Pennsylvania
2 4 6 8 10 9 7 5 3 1

For Mom, who gave me my creativity.
For Dad, who taught me about hard work.
It takes both to write a book.

Contents

VILLAIN SCHOOL
Hero in Disguise

CHAPTER ONE

New Kid in the Cave

Boiling hot water bubbled a few inches from my head as I hung upside down over the cauldron. It had been a rotten day.

The Detention Dungeon at Master Dreadthorn's School for Wayward Villains looked pretty much the same as the last time I'd been in it. That was a few days ago, when our weapons trainer, Mistress Helga, said I threw knives like a sissy, and I'd retaliated by asking if that thing over her eyes was a unibrow or if someone had stapled a dead rat to her forehead.

It was dark, except for the fires beneath the cauldrons. The cave had zero airflow, and the steam from the boiling water was making the room hot and stuffy. And making four villains extremely cranky.

"All this steam is ruining my hair," said one of my allies from the cauldron next to mine.

"Your hair?" asked Wolf Junior, who hung directly across from me. "You should see what it does to fur!" Wolf was, well, a wolf. But if you could get past the drool and the tail, he wasn't too bad.

"My dad is *so* going to hear about this!" said Countess Jezebel, who was dangling on my other side. Jezebel was one of my oldest allies. She was also Dracula's daughter, and her bite was worse than Wolf's bark.

It had been a rotten day for all of us. We'd gotten ourselves in hot water. *Literally.* It all started with the arrival of my new roommate . . .

* * *

"Rune Drexler to the office, please."

I was nodding off in History of Villainy class when Miss Salem's tinny voice rang out from the hole in the wall that served as an intercom. I jerked my head up.

"What?" I said a little too loudly. A thin string of drool dangled from my mouth, connecting to a small puddle on my desk.

At the front of the classcave, Master Dreadthorn stopped writing on the blackboard. He lowered his hand, then turned around in a way that only *really* good villains can manage. You know, like his feet weren't even moving and he was standing on some kind of turntable. Slow. Menacing. Creepy.

The Dread Master's black eyes fell on me, and for a minute I worried he would ask me a riddle and give me detention. It had happened before. Instead, he just stared at me.

"That's you, Rune," he said finally, his eyes never blinking.

"Oh. Right." I wiped my slobbery chin with my sleeve, gathered up my books, and scurried out the door.

Some kids might be scared to get called to the office. Not me. When the school Master is your dad, and you are leaving him safely behind, going to the office is like going to recess.

I hurried through the series of caves and dungeons that served as our school, past the Great Clock, past torches glowing green with dragonfire, and down another corridor leading to the office. It was a small cave with a little fireplace and wooden desk where Miss Salem, the school secretary, pretty much lived. She was about a bazillion years old and all wrinkly with white, wiry hair. She looked like a mummified potato and was about as much fun.

"You called me?" I said.

"Rune Drexler?" she asked, as if she didn't recognize me. Maybe she didn't. I don't know. She was pretty forgetful.

"Yes. It's me, Miss Salem. What's going on?"

"New roommate," she said, nodding toward the corner.

I hadn't noticed him when I'd walked in, but now I saw there was a kid with a suitcase sitting on a bench by the door. And he wasn't alone. Standing next to him was Morgana from Mistress Morgana's School for Exemplary Villains. She'd hatched an evil scheme against Master Dreadthorn's school a few months earlier, so I pretty much loathed her. There she was, looking all gorgeous and kind of fake, too, with her long red nails, perfect blond curls, and the scent of her evilness filling the room. Or maybe it was just her perfume.

She smiled at me and waved like we were friends or something. I just scowled back.

"Rune Drexler," she said, walking toward me. "I haven't seen you since—"

"Since I ruined your Plot to take over our school using my half brother, Chad?" I said.

The forced little smile on her face faltered for a minute, and her green eyes narrowed, then she recovered herself and was all smiles again.

"Let's not dwell on the past, Rune. I'm here with a new student, and it looks as though you two will be roommates. How delightful!"

My eyes flickered to the kid, then back to Morgana.

I didn't trust her. As a villain, I actually didn't trust anybody, but Morgana I *really* didn't trust.

"Does Master Dreadthorn know about this?" I asked.

"Of course," Morgana said silkily in her fake British accent. "This young man here is a transfer student. He's polite, thoughtful, and hasn't been making any trouble at my school. I don't know if there's any hope for him. I thought he could use a little time here, you know, to whip him into shape."

"Hey," said the kid, walking over to me. "Name's Dodge. Dodge VonDoe."

He held out his hand. I checked it for hidden wires, needles, and poison hand cream, then I shook it.

"Rune Drexler," I said.

It's hard to describe my first impression of Dodge VonDoe. He had brown hair, hazel eyes, tan skin, and a small scar across his left eyebrow. He looked like an average kid. But there was also something a little *different* about him. I couldn't quite figure out what it was. Maybe the tan should've alerted me. I mean, most villains don't get to the beach very often. And his handshake. It was really firm and confident. He didn't seem wary or suspicious like most new villains.

"Well, I can see you two are going to get along fabulously!" said Morgana in her phony cheery voice.

5

"Dodge, I expect to see some deplorable behavior from you. I'll review your progress reports in a few weeks and then decide if you're fit to return to a school for *exemplary* villains."

She looked right at me when she said that last part. I wanted to kick her in the shin but decided it probably wouldn't help.

"Ta!" Morgana said with a flourish of her hand as she drifted out the door. A cloud of perfume floated behind, making me gag.

"C'mon," I said to Dodge. "Follow me."

Our first stop was my room. I didn't realize how dirty it'd gotten since my old roommate and half brother, Chad, disappeared in a deluge of red frosting. Long story.

I scooped my dirty laundry off Chad's old bunk bed to clear a space for the new kid. Then I introduced him to Eye of Newt, my one-eyed pet salamander. Once Dodge had unpacked, we started talking.

"So, which parent is the villain?" I asked. The new kid looked kind of confused, so I elaborated. "You're a halfsie, right? Half villain, half human? So, is your mom the villain or your dad?"

Pretty much every villain was a halfsie: one villain parent and one regular old human parent. For instance, I was half-warlock. Jez was half-vampire, and Wolf

Junior was only half-wolf. Once they realized we were villains, our human parents didn't tend to stick around. Go figure.

"Oh, uh, my dad. He's a doctor."

"Cool! Like a mad doctor? Or an evil scientist?" I asked.

"Yeah, something like that."

Maybe this kid wasn't so bad. I started to think of all the ways he could help me in Mad Science class. We had just finished up the unit on poisons and potions and were starting a lab where everyone had to build their own doomsday devices. So far, mine looked like the deformed child of a toaster and a teakettle . . . and was just about as useful for wiping out humanity.

Instead of going back to class, I decided to show the new kid around. Master Dreadthorn's school had been built beneath the ruins of an old castle. I took Dodge down our corridor and to a main intersection where lots of hallways met. Here, at this central hub, was the monstrosity known as the Great Clock—a towering machine surrounded by carvings of fanged and clawed beasts all smiling hideously. The clock's harsh chimes were less like bells and more like the honk of a goose—a dying one, being kicked repeatedly.

To the right of the Great Clock was the hallway leading to the girls' dorms. I explained to Dodge how the girls' corridors were guarded by a set of elaborate traps and obstacles. They had been specifically built for a female villain's mind. No boy had ever successfully navigated them all. Dodge raised one eyebrow with keen interest.

"Really?" he asked, peering curiously down the corridor. I knew that tone of voice. Many a new kid had assumed that same confidence before being dragged from the girls' corridor in tattered, singed, half-chewed pieces.

"Don't even try, man," I said. "There's, like . . . poisonous snakes and flamethrowers and stuff."

"Doesn't sound like something built for a girl villain's mind," said Dodge.

"You obviously haven't met many girl villains," I said.

The girls' dorms were mostly empty, anyway, because it was nighttime, and all classes at Master Dreadthorn's school were held at night. We passed some classcaves where all the villain kids were still having lessons and continued our tour down the torch-lit corridors, past the bathrooms and through the cafeteria cave to the lower dungeons to meet the dragons, Fafnir and Custard.

They were chained near a natural spring in a colossal cavern. Fafnir was kind of old. He'd been green once, but his scales were a dull gray now. He didn't have many teeth left in his sunken mouth, and getting him to blow fire for the torches was nearly impossible. All he wanted to do was sleep with his tattered wings folded over his eyes.

Custard, on the other hand, was a vibrant golden dragon—a young hatchling who took every opportunity to pester Fafnir, blowing fire at him and nipping at his spiked tail. That was a mistake, because Fafnir's tail wasn't as weak as the rest of him. I guess you could call it his "business end." Whenever Custard was being particularly pestering, Fafnir would smack her upside the head with his spiked tail. It usually put her in her place, buying Fafnir an hour or two of peace before Custard started up again.

"You won't have to worry about them for a while," I said to Dodge. "You don't deal with the dragons much unless you're a Fiend like me. You're just a Crook." Yeah, I outranked him. And yeah, I was rubbing it in. Villains always rub stuff in.

"Well, I guess that's it," I said.

"Aren't you forgetting something?" Dodge asked.

"Let's see, the office, dorms, cafeteria cave, bathrooms, dragons . . . what am I missing?"

"Master Dreadthorn's study, of course," he said. I wanted to laugh. I wanted to tell him he was crazy, that nobody goes to Dreadthorn's study on purpose! But he looked dead serious, and *no way* was I going to look like a big chicken in front of the new kid.

"Sure, let's go," my mouth said, even as my brain screamed in protest.

We followed the winding stone halls toward the Dread Master's study, but when we got to the door, it was locked.

"He's probably teaching class." I turned to go, but Dodge leaned casually against the wall and blocked my way with his foot.

"Oh, come on, Drexler. Don't tell me a villain like you doesn't know how to sneak into the school Master's study."

"Well . . . I . . . Of course I do!" I said. "But what do you care?"

"I just figure . . . we're at a school for villains. Let's do some villaining already. Or maybe you're scared?"

The new kid was taunting me now. He was proving himself to be sneaky, controlling, and a rule breaker. He was totally cool! I could hardly believe he'd been kicked out of Morgana's school for good behavior. I glanced quickly up and down the hall to be sure Tabs, the Dread Master's pet cat-a-bat, wasn't spying on us, then I whipped out the key I'd stolen years before and unlocked the Dread Master's door.

The room looked pretty much the same as the last

time I'd been in it. Master Dreadthorn's black onyx desk stood in the middle of the far wall, facing the door. Shelves lined the other walls, filled with gruesome jars of floating eyeballs and creepy crawly things. A fine network of cobwebs was strung across the upper shelves. The *tick-tock-tick-tock* of the Dread Master's deathwatch beetle echoed in the stillness of the room. A faint, reddish light glowed from behind the desk where a glass cabinet held Master D.'s crystal ball.

"Okay, you've seen it. Let's get out of here," I said, trying not to sound nervous.

"Hold on," Dodge said, sauntering casually past me. "Is that a crystal ball?"

"Yep." I looked nervously back at the door before adding, "I stole it once."

"Really?"

He seemed genuinely interested as he moved around the desk for a closer look. I reluctantly followed, wishing Dodge was sweating even *half* as much as I was.

"Do you have a key to the cabinet, too?" he asked.

"No," I said. "The Dread Master keeps it on a chain around his neck, so fat chance of stealing that. I guess if you were good enough you could pick the lock, but don't even think of trying it. You do *not* want that kind of trouble. Start smaller, man."

Just then, I heard a noise in the hallway. It was

11

probably nothing, but I was suddenly aware that we'd been in the Dread Master's study long enough. I pried Dodge away from his love affair with the crystal ball, and in a few moments we were running down the hallway back to our room.

"That was fun!" Dodge said, launching himself onto the bottom bunk of his bed. "You've got nerve, Drexler!"

"Thanks, you too!" I said, still filled with adrenaline.

I thought Dodge was going to be a pretty cool roommate. I was looking forward to introducing him to my allies, Jezebel and Wolf Junior, the next day. It was hard to use the word *friends*, since villains don't usually make friends. However, the year before, I'd chosen Wolf and Jezebel as my co-Conspirators for a dangerous Plot. During our time together we'd battled a multiheaded dragon, a crazy gingerbread witch, and Chad, who—despite the freckles, glasses, and delicious cookies—turned out to be a fearsome opponent.

We talked a little more. I told Dodge what classes were like and which teachers were the softest.

"Stiltskin for sure is the easiest," I said.

"What does he teach?" Dodge asked, folding his hands behind his head and leaning back on his pillow.

"Spelling. You know, spell-casting," I said.

"What are some of the other classes?"

"Well, let's have a look at your itinerary," I suggested, and Dodge pulled out the paper Miss Salem had given him in the office.

"Let's see, first period you've got Stiltskin. That's good. Then there's Stealth and Evasion class with Master Igor, which alternates every other day with Mischief class with Mistress Madwit; try saying that three times fast. Break for supper—which we usually call lunch since it's in the middle of the schoolnight—in the cafeteria cave. Then Weapons with Mistress Helga. Watch out for her. Mad Science with Doctor Mindbrood—you should be good at that if your dad's a doctor. Last is History of Villainy with Master Dreadthorn. Set your watch for a *long* snooze."

He laughed. Then we talked about EViLs, or Educational Villain Levels.

"There's Crook, Rogue, Fiend, Apprentice, and Master, just like at Morgana's. Only we don't have to wear those ridiculous outfits. You know? With the berets?"

"Oh, uh, yeah," Dodge said. "I hated those dumb hats."

The berets gave all of Master Dreadthorn's students the right to mock the kids at Mistress Morgana's. It was part of their snooty dress code. If you've never

13

seen one, a beret is a kind of saggy hat. It looks like a balloon that deflated on somebody's head.

"Are you hungry?" I asked, reaching under my bed.

"Starving!" said Dodge, standing up suddenly.

I pulled out a couple of chocolate bars. I had connections with a certain chocolate-loving vampire. However, when Dodge saw them, he cringed and backed away.

"Oh, uh, no thanks," he said, eyeing the chocolate nervously.

"You don't like chocolate?" I asked, unwrapping mine and taking a big bite, just in case he thought I'd poisoned them or something. Villains do that kind of thing.

"No, I mean, I'm, uh . . . allergic," he said.

I just shrugged my shoulders and fished around for a few old gingerbread cookies I'd stashed away months ago and handed them to Dodge, who eyed them nervously.

"What? They're still good," I said, proving this by taking a bite myself. I almost broke a tooth, but it didn't kill me. Then I finished off both candy bars myself while we continued to talk.

"Like I said before, you'll have to start over as a Crook, which stinks, but don't worry. If you're any good, it won't take you long to move up."

We talked until daybreak about classes. I told him about last semester's Plot and how I'd earned the rank of Fiend. We even speculated about what it would take to invade the girls' dorms and promised to plan a raid soon. Finally, when we'd exhausted ourselves, we fell asleep.

CHAPTER TWO

No Hugging in the Halls

The next night was Saturday. We got up, got dressed, and made our way to the cafeteria cave for breakfast.

Wolf and Jezebel were already there. My plan was to take Dodge through the line and join the others at the table. However, the plan failed utterly when we were approached by an Apprentice troll who towered over us like a small mountain.

A brief description for anyone who has never seen a troll: They look kind of like humans, but their heads are tiny and mostly bald, with big, bulbous noses and pointy, oversized ears. They have arms like apes, huge flat feet, and generally look like a bunch of potatoes that have been glued together. The forest variety is distinctly tree-ish and usually easier to manage than the heartier (and uglier) mountain variety. They are always mean.

The troll smashed one immense fist into his other hand menacingly.

"I was in line here," he said to me and Dodge as he budged in front of us.

It was a blatant lie, but I wasn't going to argue. Two hundred pounds of angry troll can't be wrong.

Even if I wanted to contest the troll and risk a fight, there was no way a teacher was going to help if things got out of hand. At a regular school, maybe. But at a school for villains? The teachers would only encourage the troll to pulverize us.

"Listen up, troll," Dodge said, holding out his hand to block the troll's way. "I don't believe you *were* here in line. I'm afraid I'll have to ask you to stand aside and let us pass."

"*What?*" the troll thundered.

Most of the cafeteria had already been staring at the new kid when we walked in. Now everybody was staring.

"Uh, Dodge," I said, discreetly tapping his shoulder. "Not the best idea."

"Oh, don't worry, Rune. Our friend . . . What was your name again?" Dodge turned to the troll.

"Frank," the troll bellowed, his eyes red with rage.

"Our friend *Freak* was just leaving, weren't you, FREAK?"

"It's *Frank*, pipsqueak, and I was *not* just leaving. I

17

was just getting ready to kick your Crook behind into next Tuesday!"

Freak, I mean *Frank*, made a motion of pushing up his sleeves, which was kind of comical since he didn't have sleeves. But I didn't laugh because Frank then pulled back one of his tree-trunk-size arms and balled his hand into a fist.

I ducked. Dodge, however, just buffed his nails on his shirt, blew on them, and managed to look completely bored as he stifled a yawn. It was the final straw for Frank. The troll swung, sinking his heavy fist into Dodge's face. Or at least, he *should* have hit Dodge's face. But, by some miracle, his face was no longer there.

In fact, Dodge had moved with lightning speed out of harm's way and wound up behind Frank just as the towering troll threw the punch. Dodge kicked Frank in the backside with his boot, knocking him off balance. Two hundred pounds of sprawling troll slid down the cafeteria line, throwing tiny Crooks into the air like bowling pins.

Frank wasn't finished. He came back for another round, angrier than before. His hands opened on either side of Dodge's head and crashed together like cymbals. Still, somehow, Dodge managed to move aside, while at the same time knocking Frank's feet out from under him.

This continued for a few more rounds. Always, the troll would attack first, but his bulk and strength were no match for the speed and catlike grace of the wiry new kid. It was like Dodge just floated through the air. Finally, the troll hit his head on the cave floor and knocked himself out. The entire cafeteria erupted in cheers, and gold exchanged hands as people settled up their bets on the outcome of the fight. Dodge stepped over Frank gingerly and proceeded through the breakfast line as if nothing strange had occurred.

We made our way between tables of chattering kids (all staring openly and pointing) to where my allies were waiting. Across from us Wolf's tongue lolled, and his tail wagged excitedly.

"That was awesome! I'm Big Bad Wolf Junior, by the way." Wolf held out a paw to shake with Dodge.

"Oh yeah," I said. "Guys, this is Dodge VonDoe. Dodge, these are my allies, Wolf and Jez."

"*Countess* Jezebel Izolde Valeska Dracula," Jez corrected, holding out her hand to Dodge. He actually kissed it, which seemed kind of gross to me, but Jez ate it up. I mean, not *literally*. She was still on her mostly chocolate diet.

We talked as we ate. I told them about giving Dodge a tour. When we got to the part about the girls' dorms Jez interrupted.

"Did you see all the new construction, then?"

"No, what new construction?" I asked.

"All the girls are buzzing about it. Apparently we're getting a very important new student. Lots of added security. There's a special dormcave being set up near the end of the girls' corridor. Everybody says it's the biggest one, but I assured them that *mine* is the biggest and nobody is coming here who outranks *me*."

Just then Jez's face went pale. Well, paler. I mean, a vampire's face is *always* pale. Beside her, Wolf's eyes were huge and his tail drooped.

Even before I turned, I knew who was behind me. He wore the usual imposing black, head to toe—black button-down shirt, black pants, black boots, and the long cloak trailing behind. One might observe certain similarities between the Dread Master's wardrobe and my own. This, I might note, is purely by chance. I wasn't copying him or anything! It's just that a villain only has so many wardrobe choices. I mean, think about it. When's the last time a villain took over the world wearing sneakers and sweatpants?

"You must be Master Dreadthorn! I'm Dodge Von-Doe, transfer student from Morgana's school." Dodge extended his hand.

The Dread Master stared at Dodge and said nothing. He didn't bother shaking his hand, either. Eventually, the dazzling smile faded from Dodge's face, and he cleared his throat before sitting back down.

"My study, Rune. *Now.*"

"But it's Saturday," I said weakly.

"Oh, I'm *dreadfully* sorry. I didn't realize villains take weekends off now. World domination will just have to wait until Monday, is that it?"

"See you later, guys," I said mournfully as I pulled myself up from my half-eaten breakfast.

"I need to see you, too, Countess," he added.

Jezebel stared openmouthed at Master D. "Me?" she asked.

"In one hour," Master Dreadthorn said, then left.

I followed the Dread Master to his study, wondering what kind of trouble Jez was in. Outside the study door, Tabs—the Dread Master's cat-a-bat—hovered, waiting to be let in. Master Dreadthorn unlocked the door with a key that hung on a silver chain around his neck. The only other person who had a copy of the key was Master Stiltskin. And me, but of course Master D. didn't know that.

Tabs flew ahead to her favorite dusty, cobwebbed corner, folded her black wings against her furry sides, and curled up to sleep. Master Dreadthorn strode around his desk, placed both of his pale, long-nailed hands on it, and stared up at me. Behind him, locked in its glass case, the Dread Master's crystal ball glowed red. As usual, I was not asked to sit down. So I stood beside a leather chair waiting to hear my doom, although I couldn't think of what I'd done this time.

"Someone broke into my study yesterday," the Dread Master said.

Now I remembered what I'd done this time.

"It wasn't me," I lied. He appraised me with his sharklike eyes.

"I didn't say it was you, did I?"

I gulped.

"If it *was* you or . . . let's say your new little friend, VonDoe, or any of your other little friends, you can be sure the consequences will be . . . *severe.*"

The way he said *severe* sent a tiny but potent glass of ice water down the back of my neck. I thought about confessing right there, which was probably what the old man had in mind, but I held my ground. It was always better *not* to get caught. And I figured if Dreadthorn had any proof it was me, I would be scrubbing slug slime right now.

There was an awkward silence. Master Dreadthorn was still staring at me over his steepled fingers. I began to fidget. My eyes darted around the room.

"Um, so, is that all?" I asked finally.

"Did I dismiss you?" he asked.

"Uh. No."

"Then obviously that is not all," he answered.

More silence.

"So, um. Why am I not dismissed, then?" I asked.

His eyes bored into my very being.

"We are waiting," he said.

"Oh," I answered. "For what, exactly?"

"You shall see."

He enjoyed this. I know he did. It was a Master villain thing, making students squirm, keeping them in suspense. He sat perfectly still, just staring at me.

The *tick-tick-tick* of the deathwatch beetle was agonizing. I began to wonder if it was *my* death it was ticking for. The soft snores of Tabs grew more and more irritating, like a faucet dripping. My own breath was loud to my ears. Little beads of sweat trickled down my face. My legs began to ache. I thought I'd go mad with the waiting. And through all the long silence, the Dread Master just stared, unblinking, at me from behind his desk. How did he *do* that?

Suddenly, Tabs stopped her snoring and lifted her head alertly.

"Enter," my dad said, even before the knock on the door.

Tabs was flying in excited circles when the door opened and a familiar face peeked inside.

"Ileana!" I said with surprise. I couldn't believe it.

"Rune!" The bubbly blond princess threw her arms around me, hugging me before I could warn her.

"Ahem!" Master Dreadthorn frowned at us. But then another person entered.

"Veldin!" said Queen Catalina, Ileana's mother. Just like her daughter, she ran into the room and threw her arms around my dad. He stood stiffly and patted her awkwardly on the back.

"Ahem!" I said to him with a smile.

He shot me a look that was pure venom.

"What are you guys doing here?" I asked.

I hadn't seen Ileana or Queen Catalina since last semester, when my Plot had taken me to their kingdom. Ileana had rescued me . . . I mean *I'd kidnapped her*, and despite her ability to talk to flying animals and a tendency to coo over babies, she actually had some villainous potential. She could pick a lock faster than anybody I knew. Plus there was a whole history between my dad and Queen Catalina involving forbidden love and a bunch of other gushy stuff. Hence the hugging.

"You didn't tell him?" Queen Catalina asked my dad.

Tabs flew into her arms, and she caressed the purring cat-a-bat. I thought it was kind of odd. Tabs usually didn't purr like that unless you had a chunk of sheep liver in your pocket.

"Tell me what?" I asked.

"Mother's enrolled me," Ileana said. "I'm going to villain school!"

I remembered what Jezebel had said about construction in the girls' dorms and added security. Now I knew who the important new student was. Wait till Jez found out that someone who outranked her was moving in. It was guaranteed to get ugly. I'd have to make popcorn.

"That's totally wicked!" I said.

Ileana dived in for another hug. Her honey-colored hair brushed my cheek. She smelled like peaches. There was another *ahem* from my dad. I just looked helplessly at him and shrugged. He scowled at me anyway.

"Rune, you'll escort Queen Catalina and the princess to the girls' corridor. No hugging in the halls. That is all."

CHAPTER THREE

Passages and Underpants

Despite his warning, Queen Catalina threw her arms around me as soon as the door closed behind us.

"Look at you!" she said. "You've already grown in just a few short months. You're quite the strapping young villain!"

I blushed and mumbled a thank-you. Villains aren't good with compliments. Luckily I was saved by the arrival of Jezebel. She stopped suddenly, her eyes darting from me to Ileana and back to me.

"What is *she* doing here?" asked Jez, almost accusingly.

There was no mistaking who Jez meant. Her eyes drilled into the princess. Ileana and Jezebel weren't exactly best friends. They'd formed a temporary truce for our Plot, but I was guessing that wouldn't last long now that Ileana was at school.

"Well, Countess, I've just enrolled, so we'll be seeing a lot of each other," Ileana said.

"What!" Jez shouted.

Just then Master Dreadthorn opened his door.

"Ah, Countess Jezebel. Come in, please."

Jezebel stared at Ileana a moment longer. Ileana smiled at her and waved. Then Jez scowled at me like all this was somehow my fault and disappeared into Master Dreadthorn's study. I was going to have to do some damage control if I didn't want to incur the wrath of Countess Dracula.

"Well, girls' dorms are this way," I said to Ileana and the queen.

"Oh, I know the way," Queen Catalina said.

"That's right," said Ileana. "You used to go to school here! I want to see all your old hangouts."

"It's been a long time, but I think I can still find my way. Let's see . . ."

And Queen Catalina was leading us on a tour of the school. Of course, I already knew every corner of the place, but it was kind of fun listening to the queen reminisce. She even had some funny stories about her old friends, one of whom was my dad. It was hard to imagine him as a teenager. She'd also been friends with Morgana and Muma Padurii—the gingerbread witch who was mother to my half brother, Chad.

"And right here was where we practiced enemy

interrogation. Those were the days!" Queen Catalina said as we passed a classcave and came to the Great Clock.

"Oh," she said, "here's a secret not many knew in my day." She studied the grinning monsters, caressing each one with her fingers.

"Aha!" She pressed the eye of one ugly little imp, and there was a grinding sound. To my total amazement the clock slid aside and revealed a secret passageway.

"No way!" I said. I couldn't believe there was a hidden passage behind the Great Clock. I must've passed the hideous thing at least a gazillion times a day.

"Where does it lead?" asked Ileana.

"Let's find out," Queen Catalina said with a smile and a wink.

She took a torch from the wall, and we followed her into the passage. The clock slid closed behind us.

The dark corridor went straight for a few paces, then descended in a spiral stairway. The dragonfire torch illuminated shreds of old cobwebs, and our boots left prints in the dusty steps.

"Doesn't look like anybody's been this way in years," the queen said.

Down and around we went until we finally reached the bottom of the staircase. Here, a circular room had been carved out of the surrounding rock. It was mostly empty except for a few unlit torches and an old iron door. On the door words had been engraved.

"What is this place?" I said, running my fingers over the ancient letters.

"We used to call it the Prophecy Cave," said the queen, nodding toward the engraving. "Nobody knows for certain when the words were carved there."

The queen held up her torch, and we read:

IN THIS PLACE, INSIDE THESE HALLS
A TERRIBLE BETRAYAL FALLS.
FULL-VILLAIN SIBLINGS, TWINS
ONE THE OTHER'S POWER WINS.
A LONG-KEPT SECRET IS REVEALED
TO ONE, THE OTHER TWIN MUST YIELD.
THE TRAITOR TWIN SHALL BE BETRAYED
AND VILLAINS INTO HEROES MADE.

"What does it mean?" asked Ileana.

"Well, maybe nothing," said the queen. "My allies and I found this room a long time ago, but obviously we weren't the first villains here. Those words have most likely been there for hundreds of years. We used to come here to skip class and have little parties. I didn't give the prophecy much thought except for the fact that two of my friends were full-villain twins."

"Really?" I said.

"Is that important?" asked Ileana.

"No," I said, "it's just, you know, kind of weird. Full villains are rare. To have both a mother *and* father who are villains? And twins? That's really odd."

I noticed the queen smiling at me kind of funny. "Rune's right, so we began to worry that the prophecy might have something to do with my friends. They tried to hide the fact that they were twins, eventually going their separate ways. After a few years, nobody even knew they were related. But of course, nothing ever happened. And from the looks of this place, no one's read the prophecy in years."

"So what's behind the door?" I asked.

"Oh, let's have a look," Queen Catalina said.

We pulled at the rusty door. It went slowly. The hinges squealed in protest, but we finally managed to open it. We were standing on a little platform with a set of stone stairs leading down to our left. In front of us was a large cavern. It took me a second to recognize it, then I saw the sleeping form of Fafnir far below. Near him, Custard was prancing around and nipping at his wings.

"We're in the dragons' cavern," I said. "Wow! It's a shortcut! When I gather dragonfire, I usually have to go all the way around and down the dungeon stairs. It takes forever. This is *way* shorter!"

"I thought you'd like it," the queen said.

"So, wait a second. Does my dad know about this shortcut?" I asked.

"Yes, of course. Why?"

"And he never told me! This could've saved me tons of time," I said.

"Well, Veldin has grown into a bit of a crab," the queen said with a smile.

Considering he made life miserable for hundreds of students on a daily basis, I thought this was a huge understatement.

"Shall we start back?" she asked.

We returned to the main hallway, and I left Queen Catalina and Princess Ileana at the entrance to the girls' dormitories.

"Don't you want to see my room?" Ileana asked.

"Boys aren't allowed in the villainesses' hallway," Queen Catalina said. "But we'll see Rune at dinner, won't we, Rune?"

"Uh, sure," I said, still thinking of Jezebel and hoping she wouldn't be too mad if I brought Ileana to supper, and also hoping if she *was* mad that Ileana wouldn't *become* supper. Jez was still not a big fan of the vampire diet, but I was willing to bet she'd make an exception for the princess.

I made my way back to my own room. I was still thinking about how to handle Jezebel when I opened the door, so it took me a second to realize what I was seeing. There was my new roommate, Dodge VonDoe. Obviously he hadn't expected anyone to walk in. He tried to hide it, but it was too late.

"What. Are. Those?" I asked in horror.

Dodge just stared at me, his mouth agape. Finally, he managed to find words.

"I . . . They . . . The kids at Morgana's must have slipped them in my suitcase. As a joke or something," he said.

He was holding a pair of what could only be described as blue tights. I mean *bright* blue. And sewn over them (yes, *over*) was a pair of what could only be described as red underpants. *Bright* red underpants.

"They look like, like—" I was at a loss. I knew what they *looked* like, I just couldn't believe it. "They look like a hero's costume!" I accused.

"No way!" Dodge stuffed the offensive tights into his suitcase and slammed the lid shut. "I told you. It was only a dumb joke. Just forget it, okay, Drexler?"

I stared at him for a minute or two. What was I thinking? Of course it had to be a joke. A hero could never get past Morgana *and* Master Dreadthorn. His dad was a mad doctor, right? I was getting carried away.

"Sorry, Dodge," I said, then chuckled. "Pretty funny joke, though."

He laughed, too, and soon it was forgotten.

CHAPTER FOUR
Party and Prophecy

What's up, guys?" Princess Ileana asked as she bounded over to our table with a level of enthusiasm that would've embarrassed any other villain. Wolf Junior moved down to make room for her. Across from us, Jez was reading a newsparchment.

Over the past few weeks, both Dodge and Princess Ileana had adjusted to life at Master Dreadthorn's School for Wayward Villains. Ileana wowed everyone with her lock-picking skills and ability to talk to flying animals—including the Dread Master's cat-a-bat, Tabs, as well as the dragons. Dodge's villainous side was a bit underdeveloped, but he was making progress, too.

"I've nearly finished my doomsday device," I said to the princess. "Have you started on yours yet?"

"Yep," she answered, then began to daintily sip at

her milk, pinky extended. (It was stuff like this that made it hard to believe the princess was actually part villain.)

Wolf and I exchanged glances.

"And?" I asked.

"What?" said Ileana.

"What *is* it?"

"Not telling," she said. Then she smiled an evil grin that transformed her from an innocent princess into something much more disturbing. (It was stuff like this that made it easy to believe the princess was actually part villain.)

I waited for Jez to make a smart comeback, but none came. Jezebel and Ileana, being a countess and princess respectively, had locked horns, or *tiaras*, on more than one occasion. Normally, the arrival of the bubbly blond princess at our table was enough to start a cat-a-bat fight, but Jez didn't even seem to notice. She was engrossed in her newsparchment. On the front was a big article about a famous superhero.

"There's that snooty Doctor Do-Good again," I said, leaning in to read the cover of Jez's paper.

"Who?" asked Ileana, also leaning forward.

"He's in charge over at the superhero school," I said.

"Oh, yeah!" said Wolf Junior, his ears pricking up. "He's always in the news lately. Last month, one of his students saved some girl from a tower where a witch had her locked up. Used her hair for a rope."

"Hmm. Resourceful," said Ileana.

I exchanged a knowing smile with her. The princess and I had some experience escaping from tower prisons.

"And a couple weeks ago, another one of his students saved some comatose princess," I said. "Apparently an evil fairy clubbed her with a spinning wheel or something like that."

"Oooh. It says here his son was kicked out of hero school after failing a Quest," said Ileana.

"A Quest?" asked Wolf.

"Yeah, you know how villains go on Plots. Well, a Quest must be like a Plot for superheroes," said Ileana. "Listen."

She read aloud:

> Prominent local hero Doctor Do-Good was shamed and saddened by the recent news that his son, Deven Do-Good, failed a Quest to overthrow the sinister villain known as Morgana LeFay. Deven was a student at his father's academy, Doctor Do-Good's School for Superior Super-heroes.

Beside Jezebel, Dodge leaned around to look at the article with the rest of us. This finally got Jezebel's attention, and she lowered the newsparchment to find all of us staring.

"Do you *mind*?" she asked, giving us all a death glare.

"Hey!" Ileana said, leaning over now to read the rest of the article. "Photo on page ten!"

She snatched the paper from Jezebel and riffled through until she found the photo. "Aww. They're both wearing masks," she said sadly.

"Well, if I had a name like Deven Do-Good, I wouldn't show my face in public either," Wolf said with a chuckle. "Hey!"

Dodge had knocked over his milk right into Wolf's lunch.

"Oh, sorry," he said, but he didn't seem very sorry. He was still looking at the newsparchment.

"What have I told you a hundred times, Dodge?" I asked.

"What? Oh, uh, villains don't apologize." His eyes kept flicking from me to Wolf to the newsparchment. Sometimes Dodge seemed so confident, and other times he acted all nervous. It was almost like he was two different people.

I leaned in to examine the photo of the dynamic

Do-Good duo. The doctor's crooked nose and whiskery beard poked out from beneath a mask. Beside him, the younger Do-Good's face was also mostly concealed except for his cheesy superhero grin.

"Excuse you!" Jezebel said, snatching the parchment back from Ileana. "You know, for a princess, you have terrible manners. Reflects poorly on your upbringing."

"Says the daughter of a bat," said Ileana, with one of those fake smiles that girls get when they're not *really* happy.

"You did *not* just go there!" said Jezebel, her hands on her hips.

"I think that's our cue, guys," I said, gathering my cloak and scrambling to my feet.

Jez had picked up a spoonful of sheep liver and was about to fling it. Wolf, Dodge, and I hastily vacated the table before insults weren't the only things being hurled by the villainesses.

"So what are we doing tonight?" asked Wolf, panting and scratching behind his furry ear.

"Giving you a flea bath," I said.

Wolf stopped scratching and growled. "I'm serious."

"I dunno. I really should finish my doomsday device," I said. "It's due tomorrow."

"Oh c'mon, Drexler. You've got loads of time," said Dodge. "Let's do something fun."

"Did I hear someone say 'fun'?" asked Ileana as she caught up with us. She had the newsparchment tucked under her arm and a stain on her dress that looked suspiciously like sheep liver.

"We're trying to think of something to do tonight," said Wolf Junior.

"I know! Let's have a party," said Ileana.

"You're not having a party without me!" said Jez, running after us. She had a stain on her dress, too. Only it was a lot bigger than Ileana's.

"Where are we going to have a party, exactly?" I asked.

"Rune! What about the secret passage my mother showed us?" said Ileana.

"What secret passage?" asked Dodge. "Does it lead to Dreadthorn's office?"

"No, why would you think that?" I asked.

"Oh," he said with a shrug, "I dunno. He just, you know, seems like the type who would creep around in secret passages."

We explained to the others about the passage behind the Great Clock. I'd been using it as a shortcut to the dragon dungeons ever since Queen Catalina had showed it to us. Everyone agreed it sounded like a great idea. We all promised to bring something to eat. Then we talked about entertainment.

38

"Who has some games?" I asked, rubbing my hands together. A party was starting to sound like fun.

"I've got Conopoly," said Jez.

"And I've got Shoots and Slaughters," I said.

"I've got Commandy Land," said Ileana. "My mom just bought it for me."

"That's a baby game," said Jezebel.

"You have sheep liver in your hair," said Ileana.

"You have ugly on your face," said Jez, leaning toward the princess and balling her pale hand into a fist.

"Okay!" I said, stepping between the villainesses. "We'll all meet after last period by the Great Clock."

After the last class, I dashed back to my dorm, tossed a few fire ants to Eye of Newt, and threw a couple games in my dragonskin pack. Then I made my way to the kitchens, where I'd told Dodge to meet me.

"Okay," I said when I saw him. "I'll distract Cook while you grab some grub."

Cook was the gnarled old pirate in charge of feeding all us villains. He was big and beefy, with lots of tattoos and only one eye. But one was enough.

"Can't you just hex him or something?" asked Dodge, sounding impatient. I noticed he had been getting more and more irritable since he'd arrived. I figured maybe he was just anxious to *prove himself* and get back to Morgana's school.

39

"Uh, no! Have you *seen* Cook? We do *not* want to get on his bad side!"

I went over the plan, then Dodge hid behind a door while I lured Cook into the corridor.

"I'm sure there was a crocodile in the hall," I said. Cook had a vendetta for crocodiles; apparently one ate his cousin's hand or something.

"An' just how did a croc get inter the school, eh?" he asked, following me out of the kitchen. Behind him, Dodge slipped around the doorway.

"Um, I dunno," I said, trying not to let my eyes flicker to the kitchen door. "Maybe somebody conjured it up in Spelling class?"

"Are ye pullin' me leg? Ye know what 'appens to villains who pull Cook's leg?" he growled, leaning closer, his gold tooth gleaming. "I cooks 'em up an' serves 'em fer supper."

I made a mental note never to eat Cook's mystery meat loaf again, even as my eyes wandered toward the kitchen.

"So do ye wanna change yer story, me bucko?" asked Cook. He was so close now I could see bits of food between his teeth.

From over the old pirate's shoulder, I saw Dodge with a sack full of food. He gave me the all-clear signal and slipped back behind the door. I sighed with relief.

"Well," I said, "now that I think about it, I might have just seen a giant slug that *looked* like a crocodile."

"Aye," said Cook.

With a nervous smile, I backed away and hurried down the hall. Dodge met up with me, and we made our way to the Great Clock. Princess Ileana and Wolf Junior were both waiting with their arms full of party supplies. A minute later, Jezebel caught up with us.

"Sorry," she said, panting. "I had to finish packing. I just have such an *extensive* wardrobe."

Beside her, Ileana rolled her eyes.

"Packing?" I asked. "For what?"

"Never mind! Just hurry!" she said, glancing around. We all knew if Master Dreadthorn caught us throwing a party, he'd have us dangling over a boiling cauldron quicker than we could say double, double, toil and trouble.

Ileana found the switch and soon we were all climbing down the winding stairway. The princess took the lead, torch in hand. Before long we reached the round room Queen Catalina had called the Prophecy Cave.

"This is awesome!" Wolf Junior said as Ileana went around lighting all the wall torches.

"Look at this door!" said Jezebel. "It must be a bazillion years old. Did you see these words?" She read the prophecy aloud to everybody.

"Yeah, Ileana's mom said she had allies who were full-villain twins, but they kept it secret," I said.

Jezebel and Wolf both looked up at the mention of full-villain twins.

"Full-villain? Not halfsies?" asked Wolf. "That's weird."

"I wonder if your dad knew them," said Jez as she unpacked the games. "He went to school the same time as the queen, didn't he?"

"Yeah. Although he never said anything to me about villain twins."

My dad never said anything to me, period, unless it was something about me getting detention, or me being a failure, or me needing to scrub slug slime in the halls.

"Well, who could blame him?" asked Wolf. "Betrayal, secrets, and power-stealing all sound pretty good, but 'villains into heroes made'? That's not cool. Who would want to be a hero? Bleck!"

"Who's hungry?" asked Dodge suddenly.

I got a funny feeling he was trying to change the subject, but since I was starving, I let it pass. The conversation strayed away from the prophecy, and it didn't take long before we were all eating and talking and playing Conopoly.

"I'd like to buy two evil lairs on Dark Place and one

42

on Plank Walk," I said to Dodge, who was the Corporate Villain in charge of the money.

Dodge passed me three little black castles, but he still seemed kind of edgy, like he didn't really care about the game. I put my castles on the board. Then it was Wolf's turn. He rolled the dice and had to draw a mystery card. He wagged his tail in excitement and knocked all of my evil lairs off the board.

"Watch it!" I said, pushing his tail away and repositioning my pieces.

Then his ears sagged and he let out a doggy whimper as he read: "'Your evil scheme to tie the princess to the train tracks failed. You must pay the owner of the railroad two hundred gold pieces for derailing the train and go directly to the Dungeon.'"

"Why would a villain want to tie a princess to train tracks?" Ileana asked with a huff.

"I can think of a few reasons," said Jezebel.

Jezebel was owner of the railroad. She was already holding out her hand to Wolf for the gold. Wolf gloomily handed the money to Jez and was still sulking when I reminded him he had a "Get Out of the Dungeon Free" card.

"Oh yeah!" Wolf was so happy he drooled all over the card before handing it to Dodge.

"Keep it," Dodge said irritably. "I think we'd all

rather be stuck in the Dungeon than have to touch that card." Wolf's tail sagged in shame.

Jez's turn landed her on Ileana's property. "Pay up," Jez said.

"I've never played before, so maybe I don't understand," said Ileana. "I have to pay all of you when I land on your properties. That makes sense. But when you land on mine, why do I have to give you a tax?"

"Because we're *real* villains and you're gullible," said Jezebel with an evil smile and a wink at me. Wolf Junior started snickering into his paw.

"You're cheating!" Ileana accused. We all broke out laughing. "Oh, very funny! Prank the new girl."

She huffed off toward the stairway and refused to talk to us.

"Oh, c'mon, Ileana! We were just messing around. Come back. Let's play a new game," I said.

"How about truth or scare?" Jez asked, motioning for Wolf to clean up the Conopoly board, like he was some kind of servant. He growled at her under his breath.

"Okay. Are you in, Ileana?" I asked.

"Fine. But only if you promise not to cheat!"

"Cross my heart, hope to die, stick a needle in your eye," I said.

"It's *my* eye," said Ileana as she shuffled back to the group.

"That's what I said, your eye." I poked her in the shoulder and winked.

She pouted some more, but sat back on the floor with us.

"You can start, Ileana," I said.

She stopped sulking, tossed her blond hair over her shoulder, and broke into a big smile.

"Okay, Dodge. Truth or scare?"

"Truth, I guess," Dodge said, sounding kind of nervous.

"Um, how'd you get that scar on your eyebrow?" Ileana pointed at Dodge's face.

"From my dad," he said. "He was teaching me how to fly and—"

"Fly?" I asked.

"Uh, I mean fly-fish. Fly-fishing. Anyway, there was an accident and I got a scar."

"Like a hook in the eye or something?" I asked.

Everyone leaned in. Villains love gory details.

"Something like that," said Dodge. "Rune, truth or scare?"

I could tell Dodge didn't want to talk about it. He wouldn't look any of us in the eye and was fidgeting with his bootlace. I wondered if maybe he was lying and he'd gotten his scar in some disgraceful way, like saving someone. We all had our faults, so I let it drop. Wolf managed to scare Dodge a couple times, but most of us chose truth, because let's face it: scaring a villain is no small task.

"Your turn again, Rune," said the countess.

"Truth."

"I've got one!" said Ileana. "We know your dad. What's your mother like?"

For a moment, I sat there with my mouth open. I closed it quickly and looked away.

"I don't know," I answered.

"You don't know?" asked the princess.

"Nope. Never met her," I said, folding my arms across my chest.

"But why?" asked Ileana.

"None of us know our non-villain parents," said Jez. "It's one of the perks of being a villain. I personally would be embarrassed of my non-villain mother. If she was alive."

I knew this wasn't true. Like most villains, Jez tried to hide her weaknesses. Wanting your mommy? That was a weakness.

"But . . . none of you know your non-villain parents?" asked Ileana, astonished.

"Nope," we all said at once.

"Mine abandoned me when she saw how cute and

furry I was," said Wolf, lolling his tongue in a half smile, but I knew it kind of hurt his feelings.

His mom had taken one look at baby Wolf and sent him adrift in a basket down the river. Talk about poor parenting skills. That's probably why Wolf had a soft spot for that drowning human kid all those years ago. Anyway, Big Bad Wolf Senior found out about it, fished Wolf out of the river just in the nick of time, and raised him as a villain.

"What about you, Dodge?" asked Ileana. "Where's your mom?"

"Uh, mine uh . . . got her head chopped off," said Dodge.

We all looked at him in shock. Even for a villain, that was kind of gruesome.

"What?" he asked, playing with his bootlace again. "Construction accident."

"How did your mom die?" Ileana asked me.

"Die? I don't think she died," I said.

"So, she's still alive? Out there somewhere?"

"I guess." Now *I* was fidgeting with my bootlace.

"Don't you want to find her? To meet her?" Ileana pressed.

"What for?" I asked, feeling weirdly angry.

"She's your mother!" Ileana said. "How did you end up with your dad?"

"I don't know!" I snapped. "I suppose she gave me

up. Or maybe Dad stole me out of my frilly blue crib. Who cares? The point is I'm a villain, and this is where I belong."

I quit fidgeting with my boots and folded my arms across my chest again.

"So let me get this straight," said Ileana. "You don't know who your mom is or how you ended up here with your dad?"

"She has a point, Rune," said Jezebel. "I mean, most of us at least *know* what happened to our non-villain parents."

"Are you seriously taking her side?"

I was feeling crabbier by the second, but I still didn't know exactly why. I just didn't want to talk about my mom, whoever she was.

"No! I just think it is kind of weird you don't know anything about your mom," said Jez.

"Your dad never told you anything?" Ileana asked.

"Have you *met* my dad? He's not exactly chatty."

"We have to find out who she is," said the princess.

"What?" I asked, looking up suddenly. I was really cranky now. I mean, it was *my* mom. Why was Ileana all up in my face about it?

"I'll help," said Wolf Junior.

"Me too. I'd like to know who she is," said Jezebel.

"Hey! I know a quick way to find out!" said Dodge,

48

suddenly sounding much livelier than he had in weeks. "That crystal ball in Master Dreadthorn's study!"

"What!" I said in alarm.

"Rune has a key," said Dodge, pointing at me. "We could sneak in and—"

"Hold on! No way!" I said. "If he finds out, he'll blame me! He'll skin me alive!"

"But—" said Ileana.

"No! End of subject!" I said, standing up suddenly and dusting off my cloak.

"Fine," said the princess as she, too, stood up and straightened out her gown, but I thought she'd given up too easily. I glared at her, trying to see if she meant it or if she was just playing me.

The party kind of wound down after that. We bundled up our supplies, put out the torches, and made our way back to the Great Clock.

"See you guys tomorrow," I mumbled, feeling angry and tired and some other emotion that I hardly ever experienced: sad.

"Rune, wait. I wanted to tell you something," said Jezebel, reaching out her pale hand and touching my sleeve. "It's important."

"I'm not really in the mood, Jez," I said, shrugging her off.

And it was true. Talking about my mom had kind

of depressed me. I'd never really thought about her that much, but whenever I did, it made me a little cranky. I turned my back on Jez and stomped off to my room.

CHAPTER FIVE

A Girl Villain's Mind

The next night, I woke late to find Dodge already gone to breakfast. Quickly, I got dressed, fed Eye of Newt a few fire ants, then dashed down the corridor hoping the Dreary-Os weren't all gone. Human kids always went for the cereal first, so latecomers usually ended up eating werewolf kibble or some kind of troll cereal like Box-O-Rocks, which is literally a box of rocks. Not wanting to break a tooth or get dog breath, I picked up the pace.

I arrived in the cafeteria cave, grappled with a Crook for the last few crumbs of Dreary-Os, and found a seat with my allies. Ileana was holding a huge bouquet of flowers. I had a sneaking suspicion she'd conjured them with a spell. Like her mother, Ileana seemed to have a knack for Spelling.

"Those are contraband, you know," Wolf said, nodding to the flowers and wringing his tail nervously between his paws. "Not allowed at villain school. If we get caught with those, it could mean big trouble."

This was for two reasons. One, flowers just don't scream *evil overlord*, and two, villains are often brought down by ridiculous weaknesses—like seasonal allergies.

"Who cares?" Ileana asked, inhaling deeply. "I like flowers. This place is so bleak sometimes. Besides, I needed them."

"For what?" asked Dodge, suddenly curious.

"This," Ileana said. We all leaned in closer as she parted the bouquet to reveal a hidden object inside.

"What. Have. You. Done!" I whispered, glancing nervously from side to side.

"Don't worry. I just picked the lock. It was no problem. I conjured up a fake to replace it, too. I'll return it before he even notices."

"He's going to kill me," I said.

Nestled in the flowers was the Dread Master's crystal ball. Wolf whimpered, but Dodge was smiling admiringly at the princess.

"There's no reason for him to suspect you," said Ileana.

"He always suspects me!"

"As soon as I find out who your mom is, I'll let you

know," she said, concealing the crystal ball as Master Stiltskin shuffled by, flashing a toothless grin at us.

I gave Ileana the evil eye, but I couldn't say anything with a teacher so close. Then I noticed something.

"Hey, where's Jez? She said she wanted to talk to me last night."

Ileana, Wolf, and even Dodge all looked at one another.

"I thought you knew," Wolf said.

"Knew what?" I asked, feeling suspicious. Obviously something was up.

"Jez was transferred. To Mistress Morgana's," said Wolf.

"What?" I asked. My mouth was hanging open as my brain tried to process the information.

"I think her dad, the count, set it up," Ileana said. "She left last night. That's why she was packing her *extensive wardrobe*." The princess made air quotes with her fingers. "She's known about it for weeks now. That's the reason she was so moody."

"She's always moody!" I said.

I couldn't believe it. Jezebel? Gone! The bell rang and everyone got up to go to their classes, but I just sat at the table, stunned. Ileana patted me on the back.

"Sorry, Rune," she said. Then she left, and the cafeteria cave was empty.

The rest of that day was a haze. I couldn't concentrate in any of my classes. In Mad Science, I was called on to demonstrate the progress of my doomsday device. It created some seriously burnt toast and then showered everyone with hot tea, causing a few minor burns. However, Doctor Mindbrood didn't think that burnt toast and hot tea were evil enough for annihilating humanity, so I had to start over.

I was so depressed by the time my dad's class rolled around, I ended up forgetting to take any notes during his lecture. Of course he noticed, and gave me a week's worth of slug slime patrols on top of my regular dragon duty.

* * *

"This stinks," I said as I scrubbed slime with a couple of Crooks who looked like they'd just graduated to training pants five minutes ago. It had been a few days since Jez had left, but I was still mad at her.

"I mean, she didn't even tell me!" I said, plunging my sponge into the bucket of soapy water, showering the nearby Crooks with suds. "She couldn't even leave a note or something? Seriously! You give a vampire the best years of your life. I mean, it's not like we were *dating* or anything, but I thought . . . she . . . I . . . Dumb girls! Maybe *I'll* transfer and see how *she* likes it. I won't say a word! Yeah. Yeah! I'll transfer to an all-boys villain school in Siberia, and she can just deal with it! No-good, useless, blood-sucking chocolate addict!"

I really had no idea what I was talking about. Mostly I wanted to vent. And the wide-eyed Crooks were good listeners. Either that or they were terrified beyond words. After the halls were sparkly clean, and I'd run out of names to call Jezebel, I trudged back to my room to find Dodge standing outside, smiling a typical evil villain grin. His mood had definitely improved in the last few days. Wolf was standing beside him panting with excitement.

"What?" I asked with my head hanging. I felt like I'd run out of steam.

"We noticed you were still bummed about Jez," Wolf said. His tail was wagging. I always knew something was up when his tail wagged like that.

"So?" I asked.

"Sooooo," Dodge said, putting one hand on my shoulder. "We have an idea to cheer you up."

* * *

That's how I found myself standing with Wolf and Dodge outside the entrance to the girls' dormitories in the middle of the day. The Great Clock chimed/honked the hour. It was one in the afternoon. Except for a couple of random teachers roaming the shadowy halls, almost everyone was asleep. As the clanging of the clock faded, an unnerving quiet settled over the school.

In front of us stretched the corridor leading to the girls' dorms. It was dark except for a few weak torches that glowed green with dragonfire. At the end of the long hall, I could just make out doorways carved into the rocky walls. Those would be the villainesses' rooms.

"Remind me why we're doing this," I said, glancing around, afraid that at any moment I'd see Master Dreadthorn standing behind us.

"To cheer you up," Wolf answered, grinning his doggy grin and patting me on the back with his paw.

"It's not working," I said nervously.

"Don't worry, I have a plan," Dodge said, staring down the hallway toward the girls' dorms.

"What's the plan again?" I asked.

"To get past the traps, break into Princess Ileana's room, and get back out without being caught," Dodge said. Sometimes I didn't really know what to think of Dodge. One minute he was Mister Quiet-and-Polite and the next he was all gung-ho-let's-break-into-the-girls'-dorms.

"Why Ileana's room?" I asked, raising one eyebrow distrustfully.

"Because if we screw up or get caught, she won't try to hex us, or sit on us, or bite us like the other witch, troll, and vampire girls would," answered Dodge.

"Fair enough," I said. "But it's guarded by traps that are, you know, specifically tailored to a villainess's mind. How do we get past?"

"Hold on." Dodge reached into his cloak pocket and pulled out a folded piece of parchment that looked about a gazillion years old.

"What's that?" Wolf asked, leaning in, his tongue lolling. Dodge pushed him back so he wouldn't slobber all over the paper.

"Blueprints. It shows all the traps and how to get past them."

"No way!" Wolf said, tail wagging. I moved in for a closer look.

"Where'd you get that?" I asked, my bad mood replaced with curiosity.

"Who cares where he got it? The point is we're going to use it!" said Wolf, his tail thumping hard enough to make the torches flicker.

"Look here." Dodge pointed to almost the exact place we were standing.

"There are hidden mechanisms in the floor," I said as I examined the blueprint.

"What happens if we step on them?" Wolf asked.

"Let's find out," said Dodge.

He picked up a loose rock and tossed it on the floor where one of the trick stones was marked on the map. There was a faint whispering sound, like a puff of air, and four tiny darts shot out from innocent-looking cracks in the wall on our right and stuck into the opposite wall. Steam hissed up from where the darts stuck.

"Poison darts," said Dodge, squeezing the blueprints and glancing nervously at me.

Wolf's ears drooped as he whimpered. His tail went limp.

"Follow my footsteps," said Dodge, looking very determined.

They were probably just sleeping darts. Not deadly, I mean. After all, we were just kids. Villain kids. Sneaking out. To raid the girls' dorms and *okay!* They probably *were* deadly.

"Are you sure this is worth it?" I said, frowning at the smoking holes the darts had seared into the stone wall.

"Scared, Drexler?" asked Dodge, whose grin was not entirely pleasant.

He didn't wait for an answer. Holding the blueprint in front, Dodge began a series of movements. I followed him, and Wolf Junior came up behind. We picked up first one leg, hopped, set our leg down, then repeated with the other leg.

"Why does it feel like I'm skipping in slow motion?" I asked.

"Well, you said yourself these obstacles were set up specifically for a girl villain's mind," said Dodge.

"Do girl villains skip? I've never seen one skip before," I said.

I could not imagine Jezebel skipping. Great. I was thinking about Jezebel. So far, this lousy plan wasn't working at all.

"Who cares? Just go!" Wolf said frantically, shoving me forward.

He was panting with fear, and I didn't want his drool pool setting off a trap, so I hurried along. When Dodge announced we were safe, we all gathered around the blueprint to see what was next.

As we stepped forward, the floor began to shake, and a hidden panel opened directly beneath us. We stepped back. Soon the hole was too wide even to jump across. From somewhere in its depths, I could hear a hissing sound.

"Now what?" I asked, worried the rumbling would bring teachers running at any second.

"This is going to be tough," Dodge said. "It seems we have to sing a rhyme."

"What!" Wolf and I said together.

"Who has the highest voice?" asked Dodge.

As the only boy in the group whose voice hadn't

changed yet, I knew exactly where this was going. It didn't help that Wolf was pointing his furry paw at me.

"No. Way."

"C'mon Rune," Dodge said. He handed me the blueprints and pointed to a rhyme written in the corner.

I glared at him and Wolf. They both put their heads together and batted their eyelashes at me. "Pleeeee-ase?" they said.

I sighed.

"Fine. I'm a little villain girl," I mumbled. The hole grew wider. I could see now that it was crawling with dozens of black snakes.

"You have to do better than that!" Dodge said, stepping away from the widening panel. We were being forced back toward the poisoned darts. I raised my voice a few octaves and sang with more gusto.

"I'm a little villain girl dressed in black. All the little villain boys make me gack!"

As I was singing, the panel began to slide once more, closing the hole.

"Do I have to do this?" I asked. Almost instantly the panel slid open again.

"Rune!"

"Okay! I'm a little villain girl dressed in black. All the little villain boys make me gack! Take a step

60

forward, two steps back." Which we did. "Sidestep, jump up, land on the crack!"

We stepped to the side as I sang; the hole was almost closed. When we jumped up, the hole closed completely and we landed on the "crack."

"That was totally humiliating," I said.

Wolf and Dodge ignored me. The doorways we'd spotted from the other end of the hall were now tantalizingly close.

"You did great," Dodge said, absentmindedly patting my shoulder while he examined the blueprints again. "One more challenge."

"Seriously?" Wolf asked. "The girls do this every time they go to their dorms?"

"No, the traps are only set while everyone's asleep," Dodge said.

"Well, why didn't we just cut class and come during school hours? Would've been a lot easier!" Wolf said.

"But our chances of getting caught would have been much higher, too."

Wolf and I exchanged glances, and I just shrugged. The point of this was to get my mind off Jez. So far, it was working pretty well. It was hard to think about one's newly transferred traitorous not-exactly-girlfriend while dodging poisoned darts and snake-filled pits and singing embarrassing rhymes.

"So what's the final trap?" I asked.

"Me," a cold voice answered.

I knew that voice even before I saw him. Slowly I looked up. Yep. My dad. We were so dead.

Quickly, I tried to think up some kind of lie, some reason that three of us would be in the girls' dorms while the whole school was in bed. Sleepwalking? No, he'd never buy that. A fire? Poison? Famine? I couldn't think of anything. We were toast.

"It's not really him," Dodge said. "It's part of the trap. It's just a bit of warlock magic."

"I'll deal with you in a moment," Master Dreadthorn said, glancing briefly at Dodge before focusing once more on me. "As for you. You will march yourself straight to my study."

"Don't listen to him, Rune. It's the final test. All we have to do is walk past him," Dodge said, starting forward.

"If he takes one more step, you will be expelled, Rune!" My dad's eyes flashed.

I reached out and grabbed the back of Dodge's cloak. He stopped, grunting in frustration.

"Rune, trust me. This isn't your dad. It's just a magical projection. It can't hurt us."

"I don't know," Wolf said, twisting his tail nervously between his paws. "It's pretty convincing."

"Just give me a second," I said, forming a plan. I had to test and see if this really was my dad or not.

"I can't believe you're talking about expelling me after all the bonding we've been doing lately," I said.

"What?" Master Dreadthorn asked.

"I mean, after you gave me that birthday present a few months ago, I thought for sure our relationship was, you know, getting stronger, Dad."

Okay, I was laying it on a little thick, but I had to know for sure if this was my dad.

"I don't care about you," he said. "That ridiculous present meant nothing. This is your last chance, Rune. You will go straight to my study. Now!"

"Sorry, can't do that," I said, and stepped forward until I was almost nose to nose with the Dread Master. "You didn't give me a present, old man. And you're ugly. And you're a jerk. And you're not real."

I walked through the magical projection of my dad, and he disappeared.

"Whoa. That was dramatic," Wolf said.

"No way. That was *therapeutic*!" I said. "I've wanted to tell him off like that for years. I might go back and do it again."

"Later," Dodge said. "First, we have to find Ileana's dorm."

The doors were before us. All of them looked

exactly the same in the flickering green light of the torches—just wooden doors fastened to the surrounding stone of the cave hallway by sturdy iron hinges.

"So, uh, which one is Ileana's?" Wolf asked as we followed Dodge down the corridor.

"She's a princess. I found out the school had to make special arrangements for her to come here— added security," Dodge said, rounding a corner and stopping in front of a door that was flanked by two stone gargoyles.

"Seriously?" I asked, feeling my school pride wavering. "We have to collect dragonfire from real live dragons, and they think a couple of stone statues are going to frighten us? Besides, that one looks like an old henchman of mine."

I pointed to the gargoyle on the left whose doglike features reminded me of Cappy, my ogre-ish former henchman who only *looked* scary but was actually quite good with babies.

Beside me, Wolf stepped forward, reaching for the door handle, when suddenly his furry paw was zapped by some kind of magical current.

"Ouch!" he barked, pulling his paw back and licking at the charred fur.

"The gargoyles are not meant to frighten us away," Dodge said. "They are magical guardians set to recognize Ileana's blood. They will only admit the princess or someone who shares her blood."

"You could've told me that sooner," Wolf said, still licking his paw.

"Someone who shares her blood?" I asked. "What? Like her mom and dad?"

"Yes, or any other relative—a brother or sister, even."

"Well, that's it then," I said, turning to Dodge. "Unless one of us is Ileana's evil twin or something, I don't think we'll be going any farther."

Something flickered behind Dodge's hazel eyes. Amusement? But he didn't say anything. Instead he pulled out a vial filled with a small amount of thick red fluid. It looked almost black in the dim light.

"Tell me that's not what I think it is," I said, backing away.

"Here." Dodge shoved the vial of blood into my hand. "Once you're inside, there's a switch that deactivates the guardians' shields, but be quiet! Don't wake the princess."

"And you got kicked out of Morgana's for *good* behavior?" asked Wolf.

Dodge flashed him a familiar evil grin that was becoming his trademark.

I examined the vial in my hand, turning it in the

firelight. As a rule, villains should not be freaked out by the sight of blood, but for some reason, it really churned my stomach. I held it gingerly, as if it were a poisonous snake.

"But how did you—"

"No time," Dodge said, cutting me off. "Just go."

He shoved me toward the door. Briefly, I wondered why Dodge didn't just take the vial and go first, but he didn't seem in the mood to talk about his strategy. So, armed with a vial of what I assumed was Ileana's blood, I reached out for the door handle, slowly, ready to pull back if I felt even a tingle of the magical barrier.

I didn't need to worry. My hand bypassed the barrier and made contact with the door handle. A moment later, I opened the door and stepped inside. For the first time in my life, I was in one of the girls' dorm rooms. I wanted to savor the moment, but Dodge and Wolf were outside waiting. I could hear Dodge tapping his boot impatiently on the stone floor.

"Hurry up, Drexler," he whispered.

I reached out my hand, ran it along the wall until I found the switch that deactivated the guardians. The guys joined me in the darkness.

"Now what?" Wolf whispered.

"Now you explain what you're doing in my room," a new voice said.

CHAPTER SIX

Vanishing Villains

There was a sound of a match striking. I blinked at the brightness, and when my vision cleared I saw Princess Ileana staring at us, candle in hand.

"Is this part of the test, too?" I asked, thinking of the projection of my dad.

I reached out my fingers to see if Ileana was real, and she smacked my hand away.

"Ow! Guess not."

"How did you even get past the guardians?" Ileana asked.

I just stood staring stupidly for a second, then I remembered the vial of blood. I quickly tucked it into my cloak pocket.

"A villain never reveals his secrets," I said.

"That's a magician, numbskull," Ileana snapped, but she was smiling.

"Oh."

"So, what *are* you doing here?" she asked.

"Rune needed a little cheering up," Dodge said. "He's upset about the vampire girl being transferred."

"What!" I said. "I'm not upset about that. I was just surprised she didn't even *tell* me."

Talk about pouring salt in a wound. I thought this trip was supposed to help me *forget* about my girl troubles.

"It's okay, Rune," Ileana said. "I'm sure we all will, um, *miss* Jezebel."

"Sincere. Very sincere," Wolf said.

"Well, I didn't know her that well, but . . ."

I didn't hear what Ileana said next, though, because I was concentrating on Dodge. He was taking advantage of Ileana's distraction. I noticed him casually moving behind her and rifling through her things— her bedside table, books on her shelves. He noticed me noticing, raised his finger to his lips, and motioned for me to keep talking.

"Rune? Are you even listening?" Ileana asked.

"Of course I am," I said. "Uh, so, what do you think I should do?"

"Do?"

"About Jez. You know. You're a girl. Should I, uh, send her a gift or something?" I glanced at Dodge.

Again, he signaled for me to keep talking as he knelt next to Ileana's bed and looked beneath it.

"You'll have to do better than a gift. If you want to get a girl's attention, you need to let her know you care about her interests. What is Jez interested in? Besides biting things and looking down her nose at everybody?"

"Uh, I don't know. Uh—"

But I was saved, because just then Dodge rejoined us.

"Well, thanks, Ileana. I'll try that. You've been a big help," I said.

"But we didn't even—"

"Talk tomorrow. Gotta get back to bed. Good night!" I said, pulling the others to the door and leaving a very confused and slightly annoyed princess behind.

When we returned to the hallway, I heard the faint buzzing sound of the barrier as it was reactivated.

"What was that all about?" I asked Dodge.

"Master Stiltskin," he said.

"What?"

"Hello, boys," a voice said.

I turned to see the bent, wrinkled form of Master Stiltskin standing a few feet away from us. He was wearing some kind of old-fashioned nightgown and one of those weird nightcaps on his head. His beard trailed down almost to his feet, which were covered with fuzzy slippers. He looked like he'd just fallen out of a Mother Goose rhyme.

"What are you three doing here at this hour?" he wheezed.

"Um. Sleepwalking?" I said.

I expected us to get in some serious trouble, but Stiltskin just chuckled.

"Not to worry, Rune. Believe it or not, I was once a young villain, eager to prove myself to the villainesses."

"What? No, that's not what—"

"Now, no need for alarm. I won't tell your father," Stiltskin said with a wink. "But you should be careful, boys. Not every Master at this school would let you get away with this."

No kidding. I don't think *any* of the other school Masters would've let us get away with sneaking around the girls' corridors. Did I mention Master Stiltskin wasn't really very villain-ish? And that he actually seemed to *like* teaching kids?

"Wait. How did you get past all the traps?" I asked. I mean, let's face it, Stiltskin wasn't exactly in his prime.

"Get past them?" he asked, looking confused. "I just used the switch to deactivate them."

"There's a switch?" Wolf asked.

Beside him, Dodge pulled out the blueprint,

examined it for a moment, then pointed at the paper and said, "Oh yeah!"

When he saw our faces he added, "Oh. Sorry."

"Okay, boys. Off to bed now!" said Stiltskin.

We thanked him and ran all the way back to our rooms, grateful to have gotten off so easily.

"What was that all about?" I asked Dodge as soon as the door closed behind us. Wolf had gone back to his own room.

"Sorry, I didn't see there was a switch until Stiltskin pointed it out," he said, pulling off his boots.

"No, I mean before that."

"Before?" he asked, changing into his pajamas. What? Villains can't wear pajamas?

"All that poking around in Ileana's room." I put on my own PJs.

"Oh." He looked away from me. "I just thought since we were there, I might as well snoop a little."

"And? Did you find anything?"

"Um, just this," he said, holding out a book and grinning.

"What's that?" I asked, taking the book from him. It was Ileana's diary.

"Wicked!" I said. We flipped through and read a few pages. When we couldn't keep our eyes open any longer, we fell asleep.

When I woke up, Dodge was gone. I figured I must've overslept again. Quickly, I dressed and dashed down to the cafeteria cave. Ileana was already there eating breakfast, and Wolf was in line getting his, but I didn't see Dodge.

"Well?" Ileana asked as Wolf and I sat down next to her.

"What?" I asked.

The princess glared at me. She was wearing pink today and stuck out like a flamingo in a litter of cat-a-bats. Nobody would dare tease her, though. After she'd hexed a few bullies, most of the kids had learned Ileana was not a villain to mess with.

"Oh. I'm sorry for breaking into your room," I said, shoving a big spoonful of Dreary-Os into my mouth.

"I thought villains didn't apologize," Wolf said with a smile.

"Shut it." I jabbed him with my elbow and grinned.

"I wasn't looking for an apology. I was looking for a certain stolen item. So?" asked Ileana.

I sighed and reached into my cloak and handed Ileana her diary back. She looked surprised, took it, and said, "Where is it, Rune?"

"Where's what?" I asked, confused.

I started to think she was really mad at me or something. I exchanged glances with Wolf, but his ears were standing straight up and his doggy eyes were round and clueless.

"You *know* what!" she leaned forward, her blond curls falling over her shoulders as she poked me in the chest with her finger.

"No, I don't!"

"Oh, I suppose it was just a coincidence that you broke into my room last night, and now Master Dread-thorn's crystal just *happens* to be missing? It's not funny, Rune!"

Wolf and I exchanged another confused glance.

"But—but we didn't take it!" I said.

"That's right," Wolf said. "You were talking to us the whole time we were there."

The princess narrowed her eyes at us.

Wolf flinched away and began lapping noisily at his milk.

I tried to look innocent. And even though I *was* innocent, I felt like I looked guilty. Then I realized trying to look *too* innocent might just make me look guiltier. I started to squirm and sweat a little.

"You look guilty," Ileana said.

Cat-a-bats!

"I knew you were a villain," Ileana said, getting up to dump her breakfast tray, "but I didn't know you were a jerk, too! And to think I was trying to help you!"

"Hey, wait!" I said, but Ileana just stuck her tongue out at me and stormed off to class.

"Did you take the crystal?" I asked. "Come on. Fess up."

"Not me," Wolf Junior said. "I was with you the whole time. How'd you snag her diary?"

"I didn't. Dodge did," I said.

"He must've taken the crystal, too."

"Yeah!" I said. "Where is he, anyway?" I looked around the cave, but Dodge was nowhere to be found.

"I haven't seen him," said Wolf.

"Great. Ileana left. Jez is gone. We can't find Dodge. Who else could go missing?"

"Attention, students," a familiar fake British accent came over the intercom. "I'm dreadfully sorry to announce that Master Dreadthorn cannot be found. If anyone knows anything about his whereabouts, please report it to your new principal, me, Mistress Morgana. I will be taking over command of the school for Master Dreadthorn until he can be located."

"What!" I shouted.

CHAPTER SEVEN

Mistress Morgana's School for Wayward Villains

She's behind this. I don't know how or what's going on, but I know she did something," I said.

Wolf and I left the cafeteria cave in a daze. I wanted to find Dodge, to ask him about whether he'd stolen the crystal ball from the princess's room. And why. Not that I didn't approve, but I was *not* going to take the blame for it. More importantly, though, I wanted to know why my dad was missing and why Mistress Morgana was suddenly taking over the school.

"Morgana?" asked Wolf. "What do you think she did? Buried your dad in a shallow grave?"

"I wouldn't put it past her. Something is going on. I can almost piece it together. Something about Morgana and my dad's crystal ball and Dodge VonDoe. *VonDoe.*"

Something about his name was nagging me, but I

didn't know why. Just then Ileana almost ran us over in the hallway.

"Rune! I'm so glad I found you! Did you hear the announcement?"

"Duh," I said. "So, you're forgiving me now or what?" Princesses are so flighty.

"It was Dodge!" she said, pulling out a newsparchment. I recognized it as the one we'd all been reading, the one with Doctor Do-Good on the front page.

"Yeah, I think so, too. Although why he stole the crystal, I don't know. Morgana did tell him to be more villainous while he was here, and—"

"No, you numbskull!" She smacked me on the head with the newsparchment.

A couple of troll Crooks walked by and looked at us funny and Ileana lowered her voice.

"We have to talk," she said. "Somewhere private. Just us. Not Dodge. Meet me in the Prophecy Cave after next class!"

Then she dashed off down the hallway.

"What was that all about?" Wolf asked.

"Guess we'll find out after next class," I said, wondering why we didn't just skip class and talk now.

Wolf left, and I was just wrestling with the idea of going and confronting Morgana myself when I was nearly run over by another girl.

"What is up with— Jez!" I said. I couldn't believe it.

There she was standing right in front of me. She looked kind of crumpled, like maybe she'd slept in her clothes. She was even paler than usual and she seemed a bit frantic.

"Rune!" she said, grabbing my shoulders. "I'm so glad I found you. Listen, we have to talk. There isn't much time. If she finds me— Hey! Where are you going?"

I had sidestepped Jezebel and was making my way down the hall to class.

"Rune? Rune!"

"I'm not talking to you," I said.

"Why not?" Jez asked, following me.

"Oh, I don't know. Let's see. Maybe because you just left without even telling me. I had to find out from my allies that you were gone. I was the last to know, and I should've been the first villain you told."

"I'm sorry, Rune. I did try to tell you. Don't you remember? After the party in the Prophecy Cave? But you didn't give me a chance."

"You had lots of time before then!"

"I know. I just . . . I didn't want . . . It was—" She looked to me for help, but I just folded my arms across my chest and glared at her.

"Oh, fine!" she huffed. There was a tiny *pop* as Jezebel turned into a bat and flew away.

I felt kind of bad. Not that I hurt her feelings or

anything, just, you know, that we didn't get to talk—because I had lots of insults that I didn't even get to use.

A half hour later, I was in Spelling class with Stiltskin, but my mind was on other things. I couldn't stop wondering what had happened to my dad. And Dodge. I almost wished I'd listened to Jezebel. What if she had something important to tell me?

My thoughts were interrupted by a knock at the classcave door. A burly man in a black hood stepped in. I recognized him as one of Morgana's headsmen.

"Yes?" wheezed Mr. Stiltskin.

The headsman pointed at me with his meaty fist.

"Rune, you're excused," said Stiltskin.

I gulped. Gathering my books, I shoved them into my pack and warily followed the beefy headsman to my dad's study. When we got there, another monstrous man in a black hood was standing to one side of the door. The headsman who'd collected me from class knocked, then stood to the other side. I had just enough time to think they looked like oversized bookends before the door opened and out stepped Mistress Morgana, followed by a cloud of toxic perfume.

"Rune Drexler, come in," she said, wiggling one of her long red fingernails.

I followed her inside, and the door closed behind me. As she rounded my dad's desk, I couldn't help noticing how weird it felt to see her sitting in his place. I glanced around the room looking for some kind of clue as to where my dad might be. Everything looked the same as always. Well, mostly. In the glass case, the fake crystal ball Ileana had conjured was gone. There was another empty space in a dusty corner where Tabs usually slept. I wondered what had happened to the little cat-a-bat.

"So?" Morgana asked, pulling my attention back to her.

She was lounging in my dad's chair, fixing me with her green gaze.

"So, what?" I asked, crossing my arms defiantly. Sure, she was kind of scary, but I wasn't going to give her the satisfaction of showing fear.

"What have you done with Master Dreadthorn?"

"Me?" I asked. "I was going to ask you the same question."

"Oh, come, come, Rune! I know you've hated him for years. It's so obvious that you and your little friends have finally plotted to get rid of him."

"Whatever," I said. "This is your doing. You're behind all this."

"I think you'll have a hard time proving it," she said with an evil grin.

Ooh. Mistress Morgana was one wicked villain. I

could almost like her if she hadn't taken over my dad's school and tried to kill me last semester and . . . No. Never mind. I really could never like her.

"Where is Dracula's daughter? The one you call Countess Jezebel?" she asked suddenly.

"Jez?"

I remembered how frazzled Jez had looked when we'd run into each other in the hallway. She seemed scared. What had happened at Mistress Morgana's school? Was Jezebel in trouble? I decided even though I was mad at the countess, I wasn't about to betray her to the witch.

"How should I know?" I asked. "I thought she was at your snobby school."

"Oh, but *this* is my school now, Rune. Mistress Morgana's School for Wayward Villains. Has a nice ring, don't you think?"

"No."

"It will grow on you. I promise. Now back to class," she said, waving me away like I was some serving boy.

"Oh, and Rune," she said when I'd reached the door. "Don't try anything clever. I'm the Master of this school now."

I glared at her a moment, before dashing off. I was late for my meeting with Ileana and Wolf, and we had a lot to talk about. When I got to the Great Clock, I checked to be sure no one was looking. Then I pressed the eye of the ugly little monster that triggered the secret door. Soon I'd lit a torch and was walking down the spiral steps to the Prophecy Cave.

Princess Ileana and Wolf Junior were already there waiting for me.

"You're late," said Ileana, tapping her pink slipper impatiently. She had her arms crossed and was holding a newsparchment in one hand.

"I got dragged into Morgana's office so she could gloat at me," I said.

"You did?" asked Wolf, shivering from head to tail. "Lucky she let you out alive."

"Tell me about it," I said.

"Have you seen Dodge?" Ileana asked.

"No, he's missing. My dad is missing. Something is definitely going on," I said.

"I know," said Ileana. "Take a look at this."

Wolf and I leaned closer as Ileana spread the newsparchment on the floor. There was the article again, the one about Doctor Do-Good and his son, Deven.

"So what?" Wolf asked.

"Notice anything?" asked Ileana.

We reread the article.

"It says something about Doctor Do-Good's son failing a Quest to overthrow Morgana," Wolf said.

81

"Right. Now look at this. See anything else?" Ileana flipped to the photo of Doctor Do-Good and his son wearing their hero masks.

"Uh, the kid's smile is freakishly white, but other than that . . . ," I said.

"Look here," said the princess.

She picked up a rock and scratched a name into the cave floor:

Deven Do-Good.

"Great job, Ileana. Resourceful use of a rock as a writing tool. Excellent penmanship. You get an A-plus for being completely useless," I said. I was being kind of mean, but I didn't care. I was still ticked off about Morgana's snooty attitude.

Ileana glared at me and said, "Look again, Rune."

The princess began crossing out the letters in Do-Good's name one by one and rearranging them until she'd formed a new name:

Dodge VonDoe.

"No way!" Wolf and I said at the same time.

I looked at the newsparchment again, examining the photo of Deven Do-Good more closely this time.

"See it?" Ileana asked, pointing to a tiny scar above the boy's eyebrow. "I noticed it right after breakfast. I'd gone back to my room to look again for the crystal. I felt bad yelling at you and thought maybe I'd just misplaced it. This newsparchment was under my bed, and I don't know. Something just clicked."

"It is Dodge!" I said. "I saw him one night in our room. He wasn't expecting me to walk in. He had a hero's costume! He said it wasn't his, it was just a joke the Morgana kids were playing on him."

A closer look at the photograph, and even though it was in black and white, I knew the costume in the photo matched the one I'd seen Dodge holding in our room.

"So, what are you saying?" asked Wolf. "You think Dodge is a hero? That he took the crystal and your dad? Or is Morgana behind it?"

"I'm not sure," I said. "I wish I'd listened to Jezebel!"

"When did you see her?" asked the princess. I thought I detected a slight note of jealousy. Yeah. The villainesses all loved me.

"In the hall right before class. She looked kind of anxious. Morgana told me she was looking for Jez. I'm sure she must know something about all this. Why was I such a jerk?"

There was a tiny *pop* and Jezebel materialized from the shadows.

"I was just waiting for you to admit it, Rune Drexler," she said with a smile.

CHAPTER EIGHT

Traitors

So, let me get this straight," I said to Jezebel. "Master Dreadthorn called you to his office that day to tell you he was sending you to Morgana's school as a spy?"

"Yes," said Jez. "He suspected she was hatching an evil plan. Apparently he'd seen something in his crystal ball to make him suspicious. Anyway, since I'm such an excellent student, he chose me."

Behind Jezebel, Ileana was rolling her eyes.

"Or maybe because you can turn into a bat," Wolf offered. Jez ignored him.

"I spent a lot of time spying. It was easy to conceal myself. I learned that a superhero had been sent to overthrow Morgana and her school, but he had failed. That was common enough knowledge, but what many people didn't know was that the superhero had made a deal with Morgana."

"How did you find that out?" asked Wolf.

"I was hanging from a rafter outside Morgana's study door when a visitor arrived. It was late in the day, and most of the students were still asleep. The visitor was hooded and cloaked and escorted by one of Morgana's headsmen. The door opened, and he was let in. I stealthily flew in behind him, keeping to the shadows and concealing myself high on a bookshelf . . ."

"Do you have it?" Morgana asked.

"Not yet," the visitor said.

"Deven, Deven," Morgana said. "We made a deal, remember? When your miserable attempt to overthrow me failed, I showed you mercy. Now, you give me the crystal ball, and I give you Dreadthorn. I need it to take over Master Dreadthorn's school."

"I'm just as eager as you are, my lady," he said. "Once I have the villain Master as my prisoner, I know my father will welcome me back into the hero community with open arms!"

"So it *was* Dodge!" I said, interrupting Jez's story. "He kidnapped the Dread Master!"

"Hold on," Wolf said. "Does that mean Dodge gave Morgana the crystal ball?"

"I didn't see it when she called me to Dad's study," I said.

"And how was Dodge able to subdue a Master villain as powerful as Dreadthorn?" asked Ileana.

"Keep your crown on," said Jezebel. "I was getting to that. So, all this happened a few days ago. I sent a report to the Dread Master, but then just yesterday, Dodge, or Deven, or whatever his name is, returned. Again, I spied on the conversation . . ."

"Well?" Morgana asked.

"I have the crystal," said Dodge. "And more importantly, I've used its power and the potion you gave me to capture Master Dreadthorn!"

"Give it to me!" Morgana's eyes filled with greed.

"It's a powerful tool," he answered.

"Give it to me now!" Morgana held out her hands.

"You know," said Dodge. "Capturing a Master villain might convince my father to accept me back into Hero School, but if I had this, too . . ."

Dodge pulled out the crystal ball from beneath his cloak and tossed it casually from one hand to the other. Morgana was getting ready to hex him, but Dodge started laughing, and before Morgana could attack, he flew out the door.

"Did you hear what I said? Flew!" Jez gestured wildly with her arms.

"Well, that explains how he traveled so quickly between here and Morgana's school," I said.

"This is all my fault!" said Ileana, burying her face in her hands. "If I hadn't stolen the crystal from Master Dreadthorn's office . . ."

"Yeah, but it was Dodge who first suggested the idea," said Wolf. "Remember?"

"Yeah! Because he couldn't pick the lock on my dad's cabinet," I realized. "He was using you, Ileana. He fooled all of us. So, what happened after that?"

"Well," Jezebel said, "while I was spying from the bookshelf I got a snout full of dust and sneezed. I didn't think Morgana had heard, but I was wrong. As soon as Dodge left, she cast a spell that forced me to change back into a girl. She tied me up with an enchanted rope so I couldn't transform and hauled me onto a ship. Then we sailed straight here."

"How did you escape?" I asked.

"The rope may have been magical, but it wasn't fang-proof," said Jez with a smirk. "I chewed through it while we were sailing and flew to find you."

"We have to do something!" said Ileana.

"But what?" Wolf asked. "Dodge, or Deven, or whatever his name is, will be long gone with the Dread Master."

"I could tell my dad," said Jezebel uncertainly. We

all knew Jez's dad, Dracula, was really just a rich jerk and probably wouldn't help.

"I have a better idea!" said Ileana.

But then something happened. Suddenly I couldn't move or talk. We were all frozen.

"Well, well, well," said a voice, and Morgana emerged from the dark shadows of the winding staircase. "Aren't you all so very clever! It seems you've found me out, but I don't think we need to burden Count Dracula with your discoveries. Besides, when he hears that you're all traitors, he won't believe a word you say."

Morgana was gloating. Didn't she know *anything* about being a villain? Never monologue! It gives your captives a chance to form a plan and escape. And at that moment, I really hoped one of my allies was forming a plan, because I had nothing.

"Yes," she said, casually circling us, trailing her long fingernails over our shoulders. "You were working together with that goody-goody Deven to get rid of Master Dreadthorn. Shame on you! Helping him steal the Dread Master's crystal ball. Tsk. Tsk."

Lies! I wanted to scream, but I was still frozen.

Morgana stopped circling us and rested her hands on the door where the old prophecy had been etched.

"And to think this is where it all began. A seed of suspicion was sown here in this little cave—a seed that grew into a bitter rivalry. All because of this," she said, tracing the words on the door with her red fingernails. "And here it shall finally end!"

I had no idea what she was talking about. What did the prophecy have to do with any of this? It was about villain twins. My thoughts were cut short, though, because Morgana snapped her fingers, and her beefy headsmen came thundering into the little room to haul us all away.

And that is how we ended up hanging upside down over boiling cauldrons in the Detention Dungeon. Morgana announced to the entire school that the traitors responsible for the Dread Master's disappearance had been caught and were being punished. She did not, however, mention anything about Deven Do-Good or where my dad was now.

"All this steam is ruining my hair," said Princess Ileana, who was hanging over the cauldron next to mine.

"Your hair?" asked Wolf Junior, who hung directly across from me. "You should see what it does to fur!"

"My dad is *so* going to hear about this!" said Countess Jezebel, who was dangling on my other side.

We were bound in enchanted chains, so we couldn't escape by magic. Ileana was trying to swing herself away from her cauldron. She'd already managed to pick the lock binding her hands.

"If I can just pick this lock on my legs, and keep from falling into the water—" she said.

"Let me help," a new voice said.

We all looked up in surprise. At first, I thought Morgana had returned to finish us off, but it wasn't Morgana. It was—

"Mother!" Ileana cried.

"Queen Catalina!" I said. "But what are you doing here?"

"I'll explain later. We have to get you out of here first," said the queen.

She quickly picked Ileana's lock, and together the two of them unlocked the rest of us. We couldn't go back to our rooms. We had to find a place that wasn't crawling with students.

"I know a place," I said.

We made our way to the dragons' dungeon, where Custard was biting on Fafnir's ear as he slept.

"Thank you," I told the queen as we stopped to catch our breath. "But how did you know we needed help?"

"Yesterday, Tabs showed up at my doorstep with a note from Veldin—that is, Master Dreadthorn—saying he feared treachery from Morgana, which I can't say is very surprising. But he said he'd received information from a trusted spy he had placed in Morgana's school."

At this, Jezebel sat up a little straighter and shot a superior look at Ileana. The princess hardly noticed, though, as she was listening intently to the queen.

"I never liked Morgana much," the queen continued, "and after her attack on my kingdom last year, I warned Veldin not to trust her! When Tabs showed up with the message, I rushed here—with a little help from a few handy spells I know—hoping to be of some assistance. But just as I was arriving, I heard Morgana make an announcement about traitors and knew I was too late for Veldin. Instead I set out to find and free all of you."

"What happens now?" asked Wolf Junior, licking at his steam-soaked fur.

"Now I'll have to get you all somewhere safe," said the queen.

"No," I said. Everyone looked at me. "Now we go rescue my dad."

CHAPTER NINE

Villains to the Rescue

No, absolutely not."

We'd already formed a rough plan, but Queen Catalina wasn't going for it.

"Mother, we have to," Ileana said as she cautiously approached the dragons.

Fafnir took no immediate notice, but Custard's ears perked up as she raised her slender yellow head to fix her eyes on the princess. I really hoped Ileana knew what she was doing. Nothing smells worse than burnt princess.

"I won't allow it. It's much too dangerous for children. I'm sorry, but—" The queen began some kind of spell to stop us, but Ileana was ready. She fired off a spell of her own, silencing the queen and freezing her in place just as Morgana had done to us in the Prophecy Cave.

"Hey, it worked!" Ileana said, surprised at her own skills. Then her smile faded. "I'm sorry, Mother." She kissed the queen's cheek. "It'll wear off after we're gone."

We all mumbled our apologies to the queen. It felt wrong to hex her like that after she'd set us free and was so worried for us. She was like the mom none of us had ever had. And don't judge me. Even villains can feel bad about hexing nice ladies!

"Are you sure you can do this?" I asked the princess.

She was already cooing to Custard, and even Fafnir began to take notice, raising his milky white eyes toward the sound of the princess's voice. The fact that Ileana could talk to flying animals was kind of embarrassing, but I was willing to let it slide for now, especially since she was getting us our ride. Besides there's a big difference between birds and dragons. Just try cleaning out a birdcage, then cleaning out a dragon cave. Big, *big* difference. In a few moments, both dragons were bent low to the ground, waiting for us to climb aboard.

"Everybody ready?" the princess asked as she scrambled onto the old dragon's back.

Jezebel immediately climbed onto Custard. The young dragon snorted a puff of smoke and twitched her tail, but didn't try to eat Jez, which was a good sign to me. Then Ileana and Jezebel both looked at me expectantly. *Cat-a-bats!*

I was saved by Wolf Junior, who climbed up next to the princess with a wink at me. I reminded myself later to find an extra raw hunk of sheep liver to thank him. Then I climbed up behind Jezebel. I had no idea where to put my hands, so I folded them in front of my chest, which was pretty dumb because Custard chose to stand up and I almost tumbled off the dragon's back.

"How do we hold on?" Jezebel asked.

"Oh, here," Ileana said, conjuring reins for each dragon.

"Where did you learn to spell like that? I know it wasn't in Stiltskin's class!" I said, impressed.

"Well, my mom taught me a few things on the sly," said Ileana.

We all glanced guiltily at the queen, who was still frozen. Only her worried eyes followed us.

"She'll be fine," Ileana said, reading our thoughts.

Then the princess cooed some more, and Custard leaped into the air. With another spell from Ileana, the chains holding the dragons broke, and Jez and I were airborne. It took a little more coaxing to get Fafnir off the ground, but soon he was flying next to us in the vast dungeon cave.

"How do we get out?" Wolf asked, clutching tightly to Ileana with both paws.

But Custard was already on it. With a roar, she rushed up toward the top of the enormous cavern. Locating one of the outer walls, she swung around mid-air, nearly dislodging me and Jezebel, and blasted the rock with her spiked tail. It took a few blows, but then the wall began to crack, and finally to crumble, leaving a dragon-size hole to the outside. Soon, we were flying across the night landscape.

"Where are we going, exactly?" Jezebel shouted above the roar of the wind.

"Doctor Do-Good's School for Superior Superheroes," I said.

"But where's that?"

"Um . . . that way-ish," I said, pointing vaguely toward the west.

"You have no idea, do you?" asked Jezebel.

"Not really."

"So, what? We're just going to fly around in circles until the sun comes up?" Jezebel asked, looking nervously behind us, where the sky was already growing violet. Vampires don't exactly love sunrises.

"Hang on," said Ileana. "Men just need to learn how to ask for directions."

She cooed at the trees below us, and a flock of

sparrows all rose into the air to circle and twitter at her. One landed on her outstretched hand. There was a series of very unvillain-ish hoots and warbles. Then the little bird joined the others, and they returned to their trees.

"It's this way," said the princess, taking the lead on Fafnir, with Wolf behind her.

"Okay, that was impressive," I said. Jezebel elbowed me in the ribs, and I reminded myself not to compliment the princess while I was sitting this close to someone who could kill me with one bite.

In front of us, Wolf had lost his fear of flying and was now hanging his head to the side with his ears and tongue flapping in the wind. Little flecks of drool kept splatting me and Jez in the face.

In a little over an hour, we caught our first glimpse of Doctor Do-Good's School for Superior Superheroes. It was a silvery white castle that looked like it'd been carved out of the surrounding mountains. Yellow light spilled out from the many windows. Moonlight illuminated the landscape. A stone bridge arched over a river in front of the main entrance. Behind the castle, a waterfall rushed down the mountainside.

"Bleck!" said Jezebel. "I'm surprised they haven't built a theme park around it yet."

We circled high above looking for a hidden place

where we could land. Spying a grassy spot under a cliff, the dragons spiraled down.

"So, what's the plan again?" asked Wolf Junior, sliding off the dragon to the ground.

"We have to find a way inside, find the Dread Master's crystal, use it to locate him, then make our escape," I said, landing next to him. The villainesses also dismounted and joined us.

"Uh-huh," said Wolf. "And how are we going to do that exactly?"

"No idea," I said.

"Well, whatever we're doing, we need to hurry," Jezebel said, her eyes darting toward the eastern horizon, where the sky was now a pinkish-yellow.

"Right," I said. "Follow me."

We made our way to the river that flowed past the castle. Beneath the bridge I spotted what I was looking for.

"A sewage drain? Not a chance!" said Jezebel.

"Your choice," I said. "But it's either get wet or get fried."

Just then the sun made its way over the horizon. The first beams hadn't reached our hiding place under the bridge, but it was only a matter of minutes.

"Me first!" said Jezebel. With a *pop* she turned into a bat and flew into the drain. The rest of us followed.

"Remind me again why we're doing this," said Wolf Junior as we trudged through the stinky muck of the sewage tunnels. "I mean, no offense, Rune, but what do we care if Morgana or your dad is in charge at school?"

"Well," said Ileana, "Morgana knows that *you* know her secrets—that she made a deal with a superhero to have Master Dreadthorn kidnapped. Do you really think she'll just let you live? Oh, sure, she might not do the deed outright, in front of the whole school. No, you'll be checking your sheep liver for poison, living in fear that around every corner some kind of 'accident' might be waiting to happen—a tumble down slippery stairs, a loose stone falling at just the right moment, and *kapow!*"

Wolf actually jumped, then tucked his tail, whimpered, and said no more.

Ileana smiled and winked in my direction. Boy, just when I thought the princess was all rainbows and bubble gum, she'd say something like that and remind me she was a villain, too.

"I think I see a way out," squeaked Jezebel ahead of us.

We all slogged along until we came to the place where Jez was hovering. Above us was a metal grate dripping with foul water. I assumed it must lead to one of the castle bathrooms.

"Oh, grate!" said Wolf with a snort. "Get it? Grate."

None of us laughed. The grate was at least eight feet above the ground, and the holes were too small for Jez to fly through.

"How do we reach it?" Ileana asked.

"I thought you knew *all* the spells, Royal Pain," said Jezebel.

"I've only been at school for a few weeks, Countess Dorkula. You guys have been going most of your lives. Don't *you* know a spell?"

"*What* did you call me?" Jezebel asked.

"C'mon, girls. Focus!" I said.

It was clear that none of us knew a spell for getting out of a sewer, so we'd have to do things the old-fashioned way. I climbed onto Wolf's back and reached up for the grate. I managed to hook my fingers through it and push up, sliding it noisily across the stone floor. Cautiously, I poked my head up through the opening.

"What do you see?" asked the princess.

"A toilet," I said.

Jezebel flew through the hole. It opened inside a bathroom stall. I hoisted myself up, then reached down to help Wolf, with Ileana pushing him from behind.

"Get your tail out of my face!" she said.

Once Wolf was up, I reached down for Ileana, then slid the grate back in place.

"What now?" Jez whispered as she perched on my shoulder.

"Well, first we need to get out of this stall," I said.

Ileana was standing on the toilet, and Wolf was crammed against me. My face was smashed into the stall door. It was getting seriously crowded. But we all froze when we heard voices. Wolf's ears cocked up and turned toward the sound. A group of boys had entered the bathroom.

"Why did we have to meet so early?" asked one boy. "Everyone's still asleep." I could hear him yawning.

"We're meeting early *because* everyone's still asleep, numbskull," said a voice I recognized. And by the way my allies were all staring at each other, I knew they recognized it, too: Dodge VonDoe, aka Deven Do-Good. I tried to see through the crack in the door, but the heroes were standing just outside my field of vision.

"So, what's going on, Deven?" another boy asked. "Where have you been all this time?"

"Rumor is you captured a Master villain!" said yet another boy.

"Oh, I captured one, all right. I delivered the prisoner to my father. The old man welcomed me back with open arms," he said. "But what I didn't give him was this!"

There was a collective "Oooooh!"

"What is it, Deven?" asked one of the boys.

"It's a magic crystal ball that can tell you anything

you want to know. Like how to capture a Master villain, for instance."

The boys all chuckled.

"Yep, that warlock villain didn't even see it coming. The crystal showed me that I could put a sleeping potion in his drink, and it even revealed to me when it would be safe to smuggle him out of the castle. Then, flying him here was easy."

I could just imagine Deven flexing his arms and waggling his scarred eyebrow at his fellow heroes. What a jerk. To think I'd been sharing my room with a hero for the past few weeks! It made my skin crawl.

"So, it can show you *anything*?" a boy asked.

"Yep. How to attack an enemy. Where to find treasure. Or even how to take down a superhero like the great Doctor Do-Good," Deven said.

Silence.

"Um, Dev. I don't know if that's such a good idea." I recognized the voice of the yawning boy.

"What? Are you all suddenly a bunch of cowards now? I thought we agreed. We've talked about this before. And now, with this crystal, we can get rid of all our parents and their stuffy old boring rules, and we can use our superpowers to take over the world!"

I looked around at my allies, who were all nodding in agreement. Deven had a great idea! All that time at villain school must've rubbed off on him. Still, we couldn't allow him to do it. If anybody was going to take over the world, it should be villains. Not heroes. Besides, we needed that crystal for our own purposes: my dad was still a prisoner. Sure, Master Dreadthorn wasn't really much of a dad, but given the choice between having him or Morgana in charge, I'd choose him. I guess.

My thoughts were interrupted when Deven started talking again.

"Look, this crystal can tell us exactly when and how to strike. Here's the plan: I'll take down my dad first. When he's imprisoned, we'll tell everyone he was kidnapped by villains. Together, we'll rally the young heroes and mount an attack on the villain school! Once they're out of the way, there will be no one to stop us! Agreed?"

There were a few murmurs of consent, but sleepy boy was still unsure.

"I don't know, Deven. I mean, doesn't imprisoning your dad and taking over the world sound a bit . . . unheroic?"

"Don't be a baby, Aero-boy," said Deven. "This is for the greater good. We'll finally be able to use our superpowers for more than just dumb classes and tests. Now, all you have to do is keep quiet."

"Yeah," said another boy. "It's not like you can really help anyway, Aero."

"Hey!" Aero-boy said. "I have a legitimate super-power!"

The other boys snickered. "Sure, levitating a foot off the ground?"

"I'd like to see you try it!" Aero-boy retaliated. The other boys ignored him.

"Omnibrain, you and Vortex will help me subdue my father."

"How?" asked one of the boys. Whether it was Omnibrain or Vortex, I have no idea.

"The crystal has revealed to me my father's weakness," said Deven.

There was a gasp from Aero-boy.

"But, but we're not supposed to reveal our weaknesses. Not to anybody!"

"That's why I used the crystal. Try to keep up, Aero." It was pretty obvious Deven and his band didn't have much respect for poor Aero-boy.

"What is your dad's weakness, Deven? Lead?"

"Meteorites?"

"No! Doctor Do-Good can only be brought down by the awesome power of— Did you hear that?"

I could've sworn none of us had made a sound, but Deven was suddenly still and quiet. I could almost picture him looking suspiciously toward the closed doors of the stalls. I hoped that Omnibrain's and Vortex's superpowers did not include X-ray vision. Then I heard the sound I'd been dreading. Deven was kicking open the bathroom stalls.

Jez dug her little clawed feet into my shoulder. Beside me, I heard Wolf panting in fear. Ileana's eyes met mine. We all knew it. We were about to be discovered.

There was a loud bang as Deven kicked open another stall door. Then another. And another. Finally, he stood in front of our stall. I could see the tips of his boots just beneath the door. Then one boot disappeared, and I knew he was lifting his foot to kick the door in. I braced myself for impact, wondering if we could possibly fight our way out of this, when suddenly I heard someone yell at the other end of the bathroom. The boots disappeared as Deven ran toward the sound.

I held out one hand, indicating that everyone should stand still. We all held our breath and listened. I peeked through the crack in the door, and this time I could see them.

"Invis-a-boy!" Deven shouted. There was a high-pitched squeal. "What did you hear?"

There was a scrawny kid cowering against the

wall. He wore a low-key gray-and-white costume, very different from Deven's bright blue-and-red tights. The kid looked young, a few years younger than Deven, like a Crook—or whatever heroes called their new kids.

"N-n-nothing, Deven. I was just, uh, sleeping."

"Spying, you mean!"

"No! P-p-please. I won't tell anyone, Deven."

I got the feeling that Deven was a bully, and this probably wasn't the first time Invis-a-boy had been cornered in the bathroom and roughed up by Do-Good's gang. Even if he *was* a superhero, I still felt kind of sorry for the kid.

"Oh, I know you won't tell anyone," said Deven. "Because if you do, Vortex here will wipe Mommy and Daddy's little Kansas farm clean off the map!"

"Please, don't hurt my mom and dad!"

"Then keep your mouth shut, and get out of here!"

With a yelp, Invis-a-boy was gone. Then the other boys were laughing. I heard a door open and close. When the sound of their laughter faded, we all let out a sigh of relief.

We waited a few seconds more just to be sure they were gone, then we tumbled out of the cramped stall, stretching our muscles.

"I think Deven's at the wrong school," said Wolf Junior.

"No kidding," said Jezebel. "He makes all of us look like . . . like . . ."

"Heroes," said Ileana.

"Shh! Don't say that. Don't even think it. We are *not* heroes," I said. "We are infiltrating a superhero school to release a kidnapped Master villain. It doesn't get much worse than that."

"Yeah, or we're fighting our enemies to save our school leader," said Ileana.

"Quit that!" I said. "Now, come on. We have to follow them before they get too far away. Jez, can you fly ahead and see what Deven's up to?"

She nodded her little bat noggin. We opened the bathroom door and stepped cautiously into the hallway. Jez flew ahead. The hallway was lined with doors. From the mixed smells of sweat and cologne, I assumed this must be the boys' corridor.

"What are we going to do, Rune?" asked Ileana. "In a few minutes everyone's going to wake up, and this place will be crawling with superheroes."

I thought for a moment. "I've got an idea. Wait here."

Cautiously, I opened the nearest door. From inside I could hear the soft sounds of heroes sleeping. I slipped into the dark room and tiptoed past double bunk beds to the closet. As quietly as possible, I opened it and pulled out the first things my hand came in contact with, then returned to my allies. We made our way back to the bathroom, pilfered clothes in hand.

"No way. I am not wearing that!" Wolf took a step back and held up his paws.

"C'mon, Wolf. It's perfect for you. We have to stay disguised."

In my arms I held a bodysuit complete with a cape and oversized hood that would hide Wolf's big ears and long snout. Reluctantly, Wolf reached for the costume.

"Okay, which do you want?" I asked Ileana.

The outfits were for boys, but I thought Ileana could probably get away with any of them. One was blue and yellow and had wings drawn on the front. Another one was red and white and included a cape. The third was orange with a green belt. Ileana went for the wings, and I chose the cape.

"This feels so humiliating," I said, examining myself in the mirror. The breastplate had fake ab muscles built in, and the flowing, colorful cape just felt . . . wrong. I tied the eye mask on to disguise myself in case we ran into Deven.

"I think you look dashing!" Ileana said, emerging from a nearby stall. I had to admit, even in a hideous superhero outfit, the princess was a knockout. She tied a matching mask around her eyes and asked, "How do I look?"

"Like a freak, but that's how you usually look," said Jezebel, who was fluttering in the doorway.

She eyed us skeptically, then Wolf emerged, suited up, hood and all. He was hunched over to hide his snout, but his tail was poking out the back of the costume. Much like his father, Wolf really wasn't very good at pulling off a disguise.

"Where's your cape?" I asked.

"Don't make me wear it, Rune. Please!"

"Don't be a puppy! You have to wear it. It'll cover your tail. I doubt that many superhero kids have tails," I said, locating the red cape and fastening it around his neck.

"There. You look—"

"Like Red Riding Hood!" Jez said with a giggle. Wolf growled at her as she *popped* back into girl form.

"Here," I said, handing Jezebel the remaining costume.

"No way!" she said, turning her nose up.

"C'mon, you might need it."

"She's too prissy," Ileana said.

"Am not!" said Jez.

"Are too!" said Ileana.

"Give me that!" Jezebel yanked the costume from

my hand and went into a stall to change. Ileana winked at me and smiled.

When Jez emerged, we stood in front of the mirrors, staring at our reflections with disgust.

"It's just a disguise!" I reminded everyone. We opened the grate we'd used to break into the bathroom and hid our clothes inside.

Then a bell rang, followed by the noise we'd been dreading: the sound of superheroes waking up.

CHAPTER TEN

My Superpower

We took our first cautious steps out of the bathroom, except for Jez, who had transformed back into a bat and was hiding in my cloak. Heroes tumbled out of every door, filling the hall with primary colors, face masks, and fake muscles—no way could kids our age have muscles that big. None of them gave us a second glance. I was beginning to think we could pull off this whole disguise thing, until . . .

"Hey! You're not supposed to be here!" said a voice.

We turned to see a boy in pajama bottoms and a blue cape advancing toward us, toothbrush in hand. *Cat-a-bats!*

I was just deciding whether we should run or hex him when he walked right up to Ileana.

"This hall is for *boy* heroes!" he said, looking the princess up and down. "Are you new?"

"Uh, yes," Ileana said. "I was looking for breakfast and um, took a wrong turn."

The boy smiled his gleaming white, superhero smile and said in a dashing voice, "Not to worry, fair maiden! I can save you!"

"Well, I don't really need—"

"Allow me!" the boy scooped up Ileana, and before we could stop him, he was flying down the hallway with her, knocking over heroes left and right. In a few seconds, they'd rounded a corner and were gone. I stood with my mouth hanging open.

"Uh, now what?" Wolf whispered beside me.

We were being jostled and shoved as kids made their way to the bathrooms.

"I'm not sure," I said, wondering if I should go after Ileana first or find the crystal ball and my dad.

"Rune," Jez said from inside my cloak, "if we don't go after Deven soon, we might lose the crystal."

"How are you doing that?" a familiar voice asked.

I recognized it as Aero-boy, the hero who'd been in the bathroom with Deven Do-Good. I turned to see a kid in a yellow-and-purple costume.

"Doing what?" I asked. I noticed his feet weren't touching the ground and recalled that his superpower was levitation.

"How are you making that squeaky voice come out of your cape?"

111

"Uh . . . it's, um, my superpower," I said.

"It is?" asked Aero-boy.

"Yes, I have the power to, um . . ."

"To create talking animals using his mind!" Wolf said helpfully from beneath his cowl.

Aero-boy looked at Wolf skeptically, then back to me. "I don't believe you."

Jezebel fluttered out from my cape and landed on my shoulder. "Now do you believe it?" she asked.

Aero-boy's eyes nearly popped out of his head. He floated back a few steps, dropped to the ground, then took off running.

"Great job, guys. Way to blend in," I said.

I made up my mind that going after the crystal had to take priority. Ileana was smart. She could take care of herself. I hoped.

Jezebel whispered directions to me from inside my cape as we made our way through a maze of hallways, past flying kids, strong kids, superspeedy kids, and one kid who could shoot fire out of his nostrils.

"There!" Jez said, pointing to a doorway. "I saw Deven go through there. After that, I came back to find you."

We slipped through the doorway and found ourselves in a long corridor. At the end was a single door with a plaque on it. I could hear muffled voices. We made our way stealthily down the hallway to the plaque.

It said: "Doctor Do-Good." This must be the school Master's office. Motioning for Jez and Wolf to stay quiet, I peered through the keyhole.

"Why are you doing this?" a man said. Although he wasn't wearing his hero costume or mask from his photo in the newsparchment, I recognized Doctor Do-Good. He cowered away from someone, raising his hands as if to ward off an attack.

I couldn't see them, but I could hear Omnibrain and Vortex as they laughed.

"I'm not going to reveal all my plans to you, Father," said Deven Do-Good. "What do you take me for? An amateur villain?"

The boys laughed again.

"But I'm your *father*, Deven," said Doctor Do-Good.

"Does a father send his son on an impossible Quest? Does a father banish his son from his own school?"

Welcome to my *world*, I thought.

"You're not my father!" Deven shouted.

"But you asked to be sent on that Quest! I said you weren't ready yet. You insisted!" said the doctor.

Then Deven's hands came into my field of vision. He took the lid off a canister and several small things began crawling out.

"No! *No!*" Doctor Do-Good shouted, backing up to the far corner.

Deven suddenly stepped where I could see him. He

reached out toward his father, his hands still crawling with some kind of creatures, and Doctor Do-Good fainted.

The boys laughed again. Deven picked up Doctor Do-Good, and I realized he was coming straight toward the door. *Cat-a-bats!* I scanned the long, empty hallway behind me. There was nowhere to hide. We'd have to try to make it to the door at the other end.

Quickly, I stuffed Jez back into my cape and shoved Wolf down the corridor. We tumbled back into the main hallway just as I heard Do-Good's office door opening behind us.

"Go!" I said to Wolf, and we ran toward an alcove that held a suit of armor.

We hid and watched as Deven and his friends emerged. One of the boys—probably Omnibrain, judging from his ginormous head—came out first. His white lab coat costume swirled as he turned left, then right, checking to make sure the hall was empty. He signaled the others.

Deven came out next, carrying his unconscious father over his shoulder. He was followed by a dark-skinned boy with spiked hair and a gleaming silver costume, complete with a blue cape.

"Here, Vortex," Deven said, handing his father to the masked hero along with a set of keys, "lock him up."

Instead of holding Doctor Do-Good, Vortex summoned a wind that swirled around the unconscious doctor, suspending him inside his own personal cyclone.

"And take this, too," Deven said, handing Omnibrain the canister.

When he turned, I could see that what I'd taken for a big head was actually the hero's exposed brain, encased in a glass bubble. I still couldn't see what was inside the canister, but I knew it must be powerful to subdue a superhero like Doctor Do-Good.

"I'll meet you guys after breakfast," Deven said, pulling out my dad's crystal. "First I need to make sure this is safe."

The boys went one way, and Deven went another. We followed Deven.

Wolf, Jezebel, and I moved cautiously behind Deven, keeping to the alcoves, hiding behind curtains, until finally he stopped in the boys' corridor and entered one of the rooms.

"Now what?" Wolf asked.

"What's happening? I can't see anything in here," said Jezebel. "And by the way, have you ever heard of deodorant, Rune?"

"Hush," I said, poking her bat-head back under the cape.

"Should we follow him?" asked Wolf.

I wasn't sure if going into a room alone with a super-hero was a good idea. I mean, sure, there were three of us and just one of him, but he had superpowers. What did we have? Fur and wings and—according to Miss Smartyfangs—stinky armpits. Not really a match for a superhero.

I was saved from deciding, though, because Deven emerged from his room just a few seconds later. We ducked back into the alcove we were hiding in. When his footsteps grew faint, I ventured a quick look down the hallway. Deven was rounding the far corner, then he was gone.

"C'mon!" I said.

Jez fluttered out of my cape, and Wolf lumbered behind as we entered Deven's room. It was freakishly clean. The single bed was tucked tightly with the pillow perfectly fluffed and centered. There were no socks on the floor, no balls of paper or candy wrappers. Against one wall, boots were lined up in perfect pairs. We started rifling through Do-Good's things in search of the crystal ball.

Wolf pulled out the dresser drawers where Deven's capes were all folded neatly. I yanked open the closet door to find duplicates of his red-and-blue hero costume all ironed and hung in a row.

"This guy is creepy," Jezebel said as she popped back into a girl and kneeled to peer under Do-Good's bed. "There's nothing under here. Not a dust bunny or anything!"

"Nothing here, either," I said, ripping through the closet and throwing the costumes on the floor. "Wolf? Find it yet?"

Wolf shook his head.

"Could he still have it with him?" asked Jezebel.

I thought she must be right. Then I noticed a faint red glow coming from a crack in the floor. I knelt down and began pushing and pulling at the boards. There was a small click and the board popped up.

"You found it!" Jezebel said as I retrieved the crystal.

"Can we get out of here now?" Wolf asked, eyeing the door nervously.

We dashed out the door back into the hallway and right into a kid. We all fell in a pile, but I managed to keep a hold on the crystal ball.

"Hey!" the kid said, sitting up. I recognized his spiky hair and silver costume, and my stomach turned to slug slime. It was Vortex. "What were you doing in there?"

Up close, I could see his costume had fake abs on the front and a circular symbol with a cyclone drawn on it.

Then Vortex saw the crystal ball in my arms and his eyes widened.

Jezebel popped back into a bat and flew into my cape. Wolf scrambled to his feet. Vortex was untangling himself from his own cape when we heard a shout from the far end of the hallway. Turning, I saw Omnibrain and Deven.

"Run!" I shouted just as the air around us started to move with a rush of invisible wind.

"Come on!" I grabbed the front of Wolf's costume and pulled him after me, running down the hall and around the corner.

"Where are we going?" Wolf asked as we dashed through a maze of hallways. At first I could hear Deven and the other boys shouting behind us, but then the sounds faded. We seemed to have lost them.

"We have to find Ileana, get my dad, and get out of here!" I said. I could hear new noises now, voices and laughter and the sound of silverware clinking on plates: the heroes' cafeteria cave. "Follow me!"

I ran toward the sounds and burst through a set of double doors into a gleaming room filled with chattering, laughing superheroes all eating breakfast. Nobody even noticed us as we came in. I tucked the crystal ball under my cape. Beside me I sensed Wolf tensing up.

"Relax," I muttered to him. "There's no reason for

anyone to suspect we're not superheroes. Just act natural and look for Ileana."

We didn't have to look hard. A group of laughing boys had gathered around a table. Sitting on top, and looking totally relaxed and confident, was Ileana still in her hero costume and mask. She was telling the boys a story.

"And then he said, 'As long as we get one thing straight. You're not rescuing me, I'm kidnapping you!' Aren't villains ridiculous?"

The heroes all snorted and guffawed. I ran up to the princess, ready to grab her and dash, but we were interrupted by one of the boys.

"Hey! There he is!" he said, pointing at me and Wolf. I recognized the purple-and-yellow costume: Aeroboy. I took a step back as the other hero boys all turned to look at us. "That's the one I was telling you about. Hey, show my friends how you can create talking animals with your mind."

"Uh," I said.

There was a tense moment of silence. I knew Jez couldn't save me this time because the cafeteria was flooded with sunlight. Then Wolf ripped off his hood, revealing his furry ears and snout.

"Ta-da!" he said. All the boys gasped, and the entire lunch room went silent.

"See, Aquinator? I told you! Pay up!" said Aero-boy, holding his hand out to another hero with a dolphin on the front of his costume.

"Uh, Ileana," I said, tapping her shoulder.

"It's *Power Princess*, if you please," she said.

"Okay. *Power Princess*, we need to go. Now."

Just then a voice I'd been dreading came over the intercom. It was Deven.

"Attention, heroes! Our school has been infiltrated by villains! This is not a drill! They are posing as heroes and are dressed in costumes. Be on the lookout for a dark-haired boy with a glowing red weapon."

I tucked the crystal ball farther beneath my cape.

"And also be on the lookout for a wolf boy and a girl who can turn into a bat."

Jez squirmed under my cape, and beside me Wolf's eyes grew wide.

"They may also be traveling with a blond girl known as Princess Ileana."

"Hey," Aquinator said, frowning at us. "What did you say your name was again?"

"Time to go," I said, grabbing Ileana's hand and running for the nearest exit.

CHAPTER ELEVEN

Crystal Clear

I was wondering if you were ever going to come find me!" Ileana said as we raced down the hall. She was kind of ticked off.

"We had to go after the crystal before we lost it. Besides, judging by the group of drooling heroes around you, it looked like you had things under control."

"You didn't know that! For all you knew I could've been in some prison being tortured!"

"Can you two argue later?" asked Wolf. We'd just rounded a corner, and this hallway wasn't completely empty. I motioned for everyone to slow down.

"Just act natural," I whispered to Ileana and Wolf. Jez was still fluttering inside my cape.

Most of the heroes were in the cafeteria, but a few had finished eating and were roaming the halls, and now we also saw teachers emerging. With Wolf hidden once more inside his costume and Jezebel out of sight, I hoped we would look just like any other heroes and would escape notice until we found a place to hide and regroup. My hopes were dashed when a teacher stopped us.

"Did you hear the announcement?" she asked.

She was really skinny with sharp cheekbones and a pointy nose. Her pink costume had a bee on the front wearing a crown with "Queen Bee" written beneath it. She also wore a matching pink eye mask with glasses over the top, which looked kind of ridiculous, but I didn't want to risk underestimating her. Who knew what superpower she might have?

"Yes ma'am," Ileana said.

"Well, we're checking everyone. Name and super-power, please," said the pink woman.

"Uh," I stammered.

"Power Princess," Ileana said. "I can talk to flying animals."

The pointy pink woman looked at Ileana skeptically over the top of her glasses.

"Really? I don't recall seeing you in my classes," she said.

"I'm new," said Ileana.

"And you can talk to flying animals? Let's see it, then." The pink woman flashed a fake smile.

A strange humming noise began to rise in the air. The teacher closed her hand into a fist. When she opened it, a swarm of bumblebees materialized.

Wolf and I took a step back as the swarm grew bigger.

"They only obey me," the woman said with a self-satisfied smirk that would not have looked out of place on a villain teacher.

I wondered if all heroes were so snotty, but as the swarm expanded the thought was driven from my mind. I worried that Ileana wouldn't be able to demonstrate her "superpower" on the bees. I knew she could talk to birds and dragons and even cat-a-bats, but bees?

Ileana closed her eyes and began humming, then the hum morphed into a kind of buzzing. The bees continued to swirl in the air. They showed no signs of obeying Ileana.

"What's the matter, *Princess*?" the pink woman taunted. "Can't control my bees? You know what I think?" she asked as Ileana continued her buzzing sounds. "I think you're those villains that everyone's looking for, and you're about to feel the sting of the Queen Bee!"

I moaned. Why did heroes always have to use corny lines like that? A thousand bee stings seemed painless compared to superheroes' jokes. But then, the humming of the bees changed. The Queen Bee looked momentarily confused. Then Ileana opened her eyes and smiled wide.

"You know what I think?" Ileana asked. "I think you need to learn how to treat *real* royalty."

Ileana raised her hands and like a giant plume of smoke the bees all flew together, obeying Ileana's will. The swirling bees suddenly turned on their "queen." She backed against a wall and held up her hands defensively. "No," she said. "Wait! I'm allergic to bee stings."

"How ironic," Wolf said from beside me.

"You better get running, then," Ileana said. "I'll give you a five-second head start."

The Queen Bee glared at Ileana.

"I am a teacher, young lady!" she said.

Ileana smiled. "One. Two."

The Queen Bee stopped glaring and fled.

"Five," said Ileana, and the swarm of bees flew after their "queen."

A few heroes had witnessed the spectacle, and I knew it was time to go.

"Nice job," I said, "but we have to find somewhere to hide."

We took off once more down the hallways. More and more kids were staring and whispering, and a few pointed. Our cover was blown, and any second one of the heroes would catch us. When we reached the boys' corridor, I spotted the bathroom where we'd broken into the school.

"C'mon," I said, opening the door. Ileana and Wolf followed me inside.

"Hey!" a little kid said, pointing at Ileana. "You can't be in here! This is the boys' bathroom!"

"Beat it, kid," I said. Then I recognized him. It was Invis-a-boy, the young hero Deven had picked on earlier.

"Y-you are those villains, aren't you?" he asked. He was growing kind of hazy and translucent along with his gray-and-white superhero costume. I was worried he'd go completely invisible, and then we'd have a problem. If he escaped, it wouldn't be long before he told someone where we were. I had to think fast.

"Hey! You're Invis-a-boy," I said. His eyes widened in astonishment. Apparently he wasn't used to being recognized. I started to form a plan. "Guys! Stay back! He's a very powerful superhero!"

Ileana played along and backed up, but Wolf said, "What?"

I elbowed him. "Oh! Yeah. Right!" he said.

"Please don't hurt us!" Ileana said.

125

"Y-you've heard of me?" he asked, standing up taller and becoming a little more solid.

"Uh, yeah. All the villains know about you," I said.

"That's right," said Ileana. "You're supposed to be strong and brave and, uh . . . good. Maybe you can help us."

"Why would I help villains?" he asked skeptically, his voice sounding very young.

"We're not the villains!" I said. "Well, I mean we are, but we're not. We're just—"

"Deven Do-Good is the villain!" said Ileana.

"Deven?" Invis-a-boy whispered, looking around as if his tormentor might appear suddenly from a bathroom stall.

"He kidnapped my dad," I continued. "We need to rescue him. We don't want to hurt anybody. Not today, anyway."

"That's why you're here?" asked the timid superhero.

"We despise Deven," Wolf added. "He's just a bully and a jerk."

"He *is* a jerk!" said Invis-a-boy. "He's always picking on me! Wait. How do I know this isn't a trick?" Maybe he wasn't as dim as he looked.

"Because," Ileana said, removing her eye mask and batting her eyelashes at Invis-a-boy, who gulped and backed up nervously, "I'm trusting you with my, um, secret identity. My name is Princess Ileana Alexandra Veldina Nicolescu, and I need your help."

Inside my cape, I heard Jez's little bat voice say, "Oh brother."

"B-but we're not supposed to tell *anybody* our secret identities!" Invis-a-boy said.

"I know I can trust you," said Ileana.

Tiny snickering erupted from inside my cape. I discreetly thumped Jezebel.

"Hey!" she squeaked, but the snickering stopped.

"Wow," said Invis-a-boy, clearly amazed. "Nobody's ever trusted me with their secret identities before!" Then he stood up tall and puffed out his chest. "H-how can I help you, fair maiden?"

I had to hide a smile. Ileana was *wicked good.*

"Um, can you keep people away from the bathroom for a while?" she asked.

"Of course, Highness!" he said, taking Ileana's hand and kissing it. Then he opened the door to stand guard outside.

"And if you see Deven coming, let us know," I added.

When Invis-a-boy was gone, Jez came coughing and sputtering out of my cape and transformed back into a girl.

"My armpits don't smell that bad!" I said.

"No, this time it was Ileana making me gag," Jez said. Then she mimicked Ileana's voice, "*I'm trusting you with my secret identity. My name is Princess Ileana-Airhead-Porridge-for-Brains, and I need your help.*"

"Hey, it worked, didn't it?" Ileana asked. "I need to wash my hand." She held the hand Invis-a-boy had kissed in front of her like it was infectious and walked over to the sink.

"I don't think ugly washes off," Jezebel said.

"Have you ever tasted soap?" said Ileana, balling up her sudsy fist.

"Cut it out, you guys. We don't have time for this right now," I said, pulling out the crystal ball. "We have to find my dad and get out of here."

Everyone gathered around; the red glow of the crystal lit up our faces as we gazed into it.

"Show me where my father is," I commanded.

The crystal glowed brighter. A picture formed. It was the hero school gleaming white in the morning sunlight.

"Duh," Wolf said. "We know that!"

"Show me how to *find* my father," I commanded again. The crystal went blank. It wasn't always reliable, and it seemed to pick the absolute worst times to be stubborn. I thought maybe my dad had infused some of his own personality into it.

"Great," said Jezebel. "Now what?"

128

"Maybe you're asking it wrong," Ileana said. "Let me try." She took the crystal from me. "Show us Master Dreadthorn's prison."

Again the crystal remained dark.

"You broke it," Jezebel said. Ileana glowered at her.

"I did not."

"Did."

"Not!"

"Okay!" I said. "This isn't helping!"

"Sorry," Ileana said. Then she brightened up. "Hey! Since we're here anyway, we can try again to find out who your mom is, Rune."

"What?" I asked. "No."

"Why not?" said Wolf. "Don't you want to know?"

"I—I don't know," I said.

"Well, I do," said Jezebel, and she took the crystal. Before anybody could stop her she said, "Show us Rune's mother."

I held my breath. I didn't realize until that moment how much I wanted to know this. For a few seconds, the crystal was dark, and I thought it wouldn't work. Then it filled with glowing red smoke. The smoke parted to reveal a woman's face. It was . . .

"Queen Catalina!" said Wolf.

"No, you useless piece of glass!" Jezebel said, shaking the crystal ball with fury. "I said *Rune's* mother! Not Ileana's. This thing *is* broken."

"It will be if you keep shaking it like that. Here, let me try," I said, taking the crystal. "Who is my mother?"

Again the queen's face appeared. I sighed. Maybe it really was broken.

Princess Ileana took the crystal from me. "Who is *my* mother?" Queen Catalina's image remained in the crystal. "Okay. Who is my *father*?"

I waited for Ileana's father to appear. I'd only met King Vasile Nicolescu once last semester while I was on my Plot, so I wasn't sure I'd even remember his face. When the face did appear in the crystal, though, I *definitely* recognized it. And it wasn't the king. It was . . .

"Master Dreadthorn!" said Wolf.

"Can you do anything besides state the obvious, Wolf?" Jezebel asked irritably. Wolf's ears drooped.

"I think we've confused it," said Ileana.

I took the crystal back from her. "Show me my father," I said.

My dad's face remained. I could see he was chained in some kind of cell, but I couldn't tell where. Next to me, Ileana was muttering to herself.

"It's definitely broken," said Jezebel.

"It's right half the time," Wolf offered.

"Wait a second," Ileana said. "It can't be!" She held out her hand for the crystal. I could see her trembling.

"What's wrong?" I asked as I handed it to her. She looked at me for a minute like she'd never seen me before. Then she cradled the crystal in both her hands.

"Show me my brother," she said.

"I thought you were an only child," said Jezebel.

"So did I," said Ileana. Then the princess turned the crystal toward us, and everybody gasped when they saw who had appeared.

Me.

CHAPTER TWELVE

A Villain Love Story

We'd been sitting in confused silence for what seemed like years.

"That can't be right," I said finally.

"So, wait," said Jezebel. "You two are brother and sister?"

"Not just brother and sister. Twins," said Ileana.

"Twins?" asked Wolf. "Are you sure?" I didn't miss the fearful glance he exchanged with Jezebel. We were all thinking about the same thing: the prophecy.

"When's your birthday?" Jezebel asked.

"October thirteenth," Ileana and I said at the same time. We looked at each other.

"It's just a coincidence," I said, shaking my head. "I mean, your dad is the king. Right?"

Ileana handed me the crystal ball. She looked like

she was going to cry, and I really hoped she didn't. Villains are not good with things like emotions and tears. I looked down at the glowing red crystal, where the image of my face was fading away.

"It just can't be," I said. "I mean, how did this all happen? How did I end up at villain school when Ileana ended up with Queen Catalina?"

To my amazement, the crystal ball glowed brighter, and a scene unfolded. Everyone leaned over to look at it. Then something really weird happened. Instead of just watching the crystal, it was like we were inside it.

* * *

"Veldin! Congratulations!"

A beautiful teenage girl with honey-colored hair bounded up to a trio of villain kids and wrapped her arms around a young warlock who looked kind of like me. It was my father.

I expected him to stiffen or push her away, but to my utter amazement he picked her up and swung her in a circle.

"Cat!" he said, and smiled. My dad actually *smiled*. Like he was happy or something. Obviously, the pretty girl was Queen Catalina.

Behind him, I could see another villain girl with bright green eyes and red lips. Her hair was almost black instead of the usual blond, so it took me a moment to recognize her: Morgana. She rolled her eyes and applied even more red lipstick.

Beside Morgana, a pretty girl with short curly hair and a sprinkling of freckles was scowling at my dad and Queen Catalina. She looked kind of familiar, but I couldn't say why. The queen noticed the girl and pulled away from my dad, blushing.

"Oh, hi, Morg! Hi, Muma!"

Then I realized why the girl looked familiar: curly hair, freckles. She looked like Chad, my half brother. This was Muma Padurii, the old gingerbread witch, as a teenager!

"Congratulations for what, Cat?" asked Muma. I could tell she was seething with jealousy, but my dad and Queen Catalina seemed oblivious.

"Well, graduation is just around the corner, and Veldin's in the lead for Villaindictorian! He's the smartest villain at Master Stiltskin's school!" said Queen Catalina, bubbling over with pride.

"Is that what you heard?" asked Morgana, not looking up from her mirror.

"And I heard you're right behind him, Morg!" the queen said. "Congrats to you, too."

"It's not decided yet," Morgana said. "We still have to turn in our final projects."

"Right," said Catalina. "Well, good luck. To you both."

She pecked my dad on the cheek and bounced away.

"How can you stand her, Veldin?" asked Muma. "She's so, so . . . unvillain-ish!"

The scene grew hazy. A red smoke seemed to fill my vision. When it cleared, the scene had changed. I was no longer looking at the corridor, but at the Prophecy Cave.

"How is that going to help, Morgana?" asked Muma. She was pacing back and forth in front of the door carved with the ancient words of the prophecy. Morgana leaned against the stone wall, filing her long red fingernails.

"Trust me, Muma. Once Cat sees he's not the smartest villain in the school, she'll dump him," said Morgana. "Then you can have him all to yourself."

"Well—"

"All you have to do is sabotage his final project. Then I'll be named Villaindictorian, and Cat won't be able to stand the sight of him."

"All right. I'll do it," said Muma.

More smoke filled my vision. Again it cleared, showing a classcave. At the front was Master Stiltskin. His beard wasn't completely gray; it had some reddish brown streaks in it, but he still looked old and bent and smiled his familiar toothless grin.

"Wonderful, Morgana!" he was saying as Morgana sat down at her desk. "Well, I'd say that puts you and Veldin neck and neck for Villaindictorian! And speaking of which! Veldin? You're up next."

My dad walked to the front of the classcave. In his hands he held something covered with a cloth. He set it on a desk and pulled off the cloth with a grand *swoosh* like a stage magician. Beneath was an odd-looking mishmash of metal tubes and wires.

"Prepare to be amazed!" my dad said. There was a dramatic pause. Then he flipped a little red switch on the side of the device. Nothing happened.

"What?" he asked, flipping the switch again and again. My dad looked up. "I . . . I don't understand. It worked perfectly last night!"

From the side of the classcave, Master Stiltskin frowned sympathetically. I scanned the room and noticed all the other villains whispering and looking confused. Except one. Morgana was smiling.

"I'm sorry, Veldin," said Master Stiltskin. "I'm afraid you will not receive credit for your final project."

More smoke. This time the scene revealed my dad and Queen Cat in the Prophecy Cave.

"Don't be ridiculous, Veldin!" said the queen. "I

don't care if you're Villaindictorian. You're the evil mastermind of my dreams!"

My dad smiled and hugged her. Then he got down on one knee and pulled out a black rose from beneath his cloak.

"Princess Catalina Alexandra Runa Dragos, will you marry me?" he asked.

She took the rose, running her fingertips lightly over the thorns. "Yes!" she said. They threw their arms around each other.

"I have something else for you," he said, reaching into his cloak again. He pulled out a tiny sleeping kitten.

Queen Catalina gasped and took the little black cat in her hand. It stretched and yawned, revealing the tiny batwings attached to its sides.

"Her name is Tabs," my dad said.

"I love her!" the queen said, cradling the kitten and rubbing its soft fur against her cheek. "I can't believe I'm going to be Mrs. Veldin Drexler! Wait, maybe not. Have you chosen your villain name yet?"

"Not yet," said my dad.

"Hmm," Catalina said, turning the black rose in her hands. "I like Dreadthorn. It has a nice ring to it."

Then I noticed a figure lurking in the dark stairway behind them. It was Muma Padurii. Angry tears spilled from her blue eyes. She ran up the stairway and disappeared.

Again the scene shifted. This time, it opened on an image of Catalina crying. She was sitting in a chair, and Tabs was curled up in her lap, asleep. Catalina's hands covered her eyes as she sobbed, and I noticed a ring on her finger.

"He can't do this!" my dad said. He was pacing back and forth angrily. "How did he even find out?"

"I don't know, Veldin. And it doesn't matter. He's my father, and he's the king. He says without his blessing, the marriage wasn't legal. We can't be together anymore. I'm to return home in a few hours."

"I won't let you," my dad said, stopping suddenly. "I won't!" He crossed the room and stood in front of the queen.

"It's over, Veldin," Queen Catalina said, rubbing at her red, teary eyes.

"Run away with me, Cat!" he said, taking both her hands in his. He had kind of a wild, crazy look in his eyes. I'd never seen my dad looking so emotional.

"No," said Catalina. "I've already agreed to marry another. Don't you understand? My father would kill you to protect me."

"You can't marry another. You're my wife," my dad said, holding up his finger to reveal a gold wedding band.

Queen Catalina wiped her eyes on her sleeve and stood up, holding her chin proudly. Tabs flew up into the air, landing on the queen's shoulder as Catalina gently hugged my father. Then the queen slipped the ring from her finger, handed it to my dad, and said, "Not anymore."

Again the scene changed. Muma Padurii stood next to my dad watching a carriage disappear into the distance. In his arms, my dad was holding the tiny cat-a-bat.

"You don't need her, Veldin. There are plenty of villainesses who would dominate the world with you!"

"No!" Veldin said, glaring at Muma Padurii. "She's the only one! I'll never love another. Do you understand, Padurii? Never!"

With a swish of his cloak, my dad returned to the school, leaving Muma Padurii behind. She watched him go. Then she spoke to herself.

"Well, if she's the only one you'll notice, then so be it!"

I heard her muttering words to herself. A spell. There was a flash of light, and when it faded, Muma was still standing there, wearing the same clothes, but her features had changed. She no longer looked like herself with the short curly hair and freckles. She looked like Queen Catalina.

I watched as she entered the school and walked

down to the boys' corridor. She knocked on a door, and my dad opened it.

"Cat!" he said, rushing out to hug Padurii. "But how?"

"I decided to stay!" she said. "I want to Plot with you forever!"

More red smoke blotted out the picture. I could tell some time had passed in the next scene, a few weeks maybe. Tabs was flying around my dad. She looked a little older, but still a kitten. My dad was holding Queen Catalina's hand and walking down a torch-lit corridor, but I knew it wasn't Cat. It was Padurii in disguise.

"You seem so different lately, Cat," my dad said.

"Oh?" asked Padurii. "Well, I . . . uh . . . I've been worried about my father."

"Don't worry. If anyone comes for you, I'll take care of them," he said darkly.

Then a tinny voice announced, "Veldin Drexler to the office." I recognized it as Miss Salem, the current school secretary. Man, she was old.

"I'll go with you," said Padurii.

When they arrived at the office, Miss Salem handed my dad a note. It was sealed with wax. He broke the seal and read the letter as he and Padurii walked back down the hall together. Even though he read to himself, I knew what the letter said. It was like I could hear the words in his mind:

My Dearest Veldin,

I've missed you so much these past few weeks. You have no idea how hard it was to leave, but I knew I had to. My father would not have stopped hunting you if we'd run away together. As it is, I've been able to settle into my role as future queen of my kingdom. The man my father arranged for me to marry is no substitute for you. He is kind and good and honorable, but I am trying to love him anyway.

I have two pieces of news that I knew I must tell you. First, the royal doctor has discovered that I am to have a child. And although you are no longer my husband, I want you to know I shall name our baby after you. I am only sorry that he (or she) will not know you as his (or her) father.

The second piece of news I have for you is that I found out how my father discovered that I was at villain school and that you and I had secretly married. It was Padurii. She wrote to my father and betrayed us. I only tell you this because I fear she might be using treachery on you some way now that I am gone.

Be well, my darling, and know that I will always love you.

Yours,
Cat

I had watched my father's face as he read the letter. At first he'd looked confused, then his eyes widened with understanding. Finally, the tiny vein in his left temple began to throb dangerously.

"What is it, my love?" asked Padurii.

My father raised his eyes slowly to Padurii's face. It was the Master Dreadthorn I knew. All the mushy, lovey, gooeyness was gone.

"You!" he said, backing away from Padurii.

"Veldin, what's wrong?" she asked, reaching out to touch his shoulder. He pushed her hand away.

"Treachery! You're not Cat. You're Padurii!" Then he cast a spell. I'd never heard it before, but when he was finished, Padurii's disguise was gone.

Fear and confusion clouded her features as she reached up to touch her hair and face. Then she realized her spell had been broken. Tabs was perched on my dad's shoulder and hissing at Padurii.

"Veldin, I can explain!" Muma Padurii said, reaching out for my father. He backed away, his black eyes flashing with anger.

"Get out! I never want to see you again!" he shouted.

Turning his back, he began to walk down the hallway. Behind him, I could see Muma Padurii's face. Her tears gave way suddenly to an insane rage. I could hear her whispering a spell. I wanted to shout to my father to watch out, but I wasn't even really there. I was just watching something that had happened before I was born.

Still, my father seemed to sense something. He turned, and I realized he'd been Spelling, too. At the moment Padurii unleashed her spell, my father completed his. I could feel the energy as the two forces collided in the air. But my father's spell was more powerful. Padurii's own hex exploded in her face. She raised her arms to shield herself, but it was no use. When she lowered them, my father gasped.

She was no longer the cute, curly-haired freckled girl, but an ugly, bent old woman. Again, she raised her hands to her face, feeling the wrinkles. She held her hands out to examine them. They were knobby and spotted with veins like worms.

"What have you done!" she shouted. Her voice was shaky and hoarse.

"You did this to yourself," my father said.

"I hate you for this, Veldin Drexler! I hate you forever!" she screeched, then fled.

I thought that would be the end of the crystal's vision, but it wasn't. There was one more scene, one final story that needed to be told. When the smoke cleared, I saw a woman in a royal bedchamber. In her arms were two bundled babies, one wrapped in a pink blanket, the other in blue.

She was alone, sitting in the bed, rocking both

of her children. Suddenly she looked up, and I saw a cloaked figure standing on her balcony.

"You came," she said with a smile, but it was a sad smile.

Then the figure entered the room and stood at her side. When he lowered his hood, I saw it was my father. He didn't return Catalina's smile, though. He looked older, and I could tell he would never be that smiling young villain again.

He sat beside Queen Catalina, and she handed both the bundles to him.

"What are their names?" he asked.

"This one," she said, pointing to the baby in the pink blanket, "is Princess Ileana Alexandra Veldina Nicolescu."

"Nicolescu? Is that your . . . your husband's name?" my father asked. The queen nodded.

"And *Veldina* is for her father," she said. "I told you I'd name my child after you."

"And the boy?" my father asked, nodding toward the blue blanket.

"I thought you should name him," said Cat, and my father looked surprised. "It's why I asked you to come. My father won't allow me to keep a boy. Only a girl. You must take him with you, Veldin." A tear ran down the queen's cheek. My father wiped it away and nodded.

"I will call him Rune," he said. "Rune Toma Emilian Drexler."

Then he took one last look at the baby girl and handed her back to the queen. She, in turn, planted a final kiss on the baby boy's cheek—my cheek—and my father took me away to be raised as a villain.

CHAPTER THIRTEEN

Double Trouble

The crystal went dark. Everyone blinked their eyes as if they'd just awoken from a dream. I had no idea how much time had passed. It felt like days, but I could still hear superheroes outside the bathroom, beginning their school day.

"Wow," Wolf said, looking from me to Ileana and back to me.

"So you guys are related!" Jezebel said, a broad smile spreading across her face. "That's great! Twins!"

I thought she seemed a little overenthusiastic, but since this officially dropped Ileana out of the running as my potential girlfriend, I'm sure Jez was psyched.

"Not just twins," said Wolf, "full-villain twins!"

Again, there was an awkward silence as we all remembered the words of the prophecy.

"Hey! I just thought of something," Wolf said to break the tension. "If you were related to Ileana this whole time, Dodge, er, I mean Deven, never needed to give you that vial of the princess's blood to get past her room guardians that night we raided the girls' dorms."

"What about my blood?" Ileana asked.

"He knew," I said, remembering the funny look he'd given me outside Ileana's door. "Morgana must have told him I was Ileana's brother. She knew, too. That wasn't Ileana's real blood."

"Wait," said Jez, "you guys raided the girls' dorms?"

"Focus, please," I said.

"Right," answered Jezebel. "So, full-villain twins."

"Like in the prophecy," I said, finally admitting it.

"Yeah, how did that go again?" asked Wolf.

Ileana recited:

"In this place, inside these halls
A terrible betrayal falls.
Full-villain siblings, twins
One the other's power wins.
A long-kept secret is revealed
To one, the other twin must yield.
The traitor twin shall be betrayed
And villains into heroes made."

It really didn't surprise me that she had it memorized. She was pretty smart, after all. I guess she got that from her, uh . . . *our* mother.

"So," said Wolf, "what does that mean exactly?" He looked from me to Jezebel to Ileana.

"It means one of them will betray the other," said Jezebel, eyeing Ileana meaningfully.

"No, it doesn't!" Ileana said. "That prophecy could be about *any* full-villain twins. It could've already happened a hundred years ago. It might not even be a real prophecy at all, just some graffiti on an old door."

"Or," said Jezebel, crossing her arms, "it could mean you're going to betray Rune."

"Why me?" Ileana asked. "Maybe it's Rune who's the traitor." She pointed an accusing finger at me.

"What?" I asked, standing suddenly to my feet. "I was raised a villain! And villains stick together, er . . . at least as long as it's beneficial. Anyway, if anyone's going to betray us to the heroes, it'll be you, *Power Princess*!"

"Oh, nice," said Ileana, also standing. "We find out that our parents lied to us, that we're actually brother and sister, and the first thing you do is turn on me?"

"Well," said Wolf, "according to that prophecy thing, it was bound to happen."

"Shut it, Wolf!" Ileana and I both said at the same time.

"This isn't getting us anywhere," I said. "We still have to find my dad."

"*Our* dad," said Ileana, raising her eyes to mine.

"Right," I said, looking away.

"Rune, don't you want to talk about—" began Ileana.

"Anyway, we have to find the Dread Master and get out of here," I interrupted. Everything we'd seen in the crystal was just too overwhelming. I was in no mood to talk about it, so I changed the subject. "The question is: Where is he?"

Of course, this time the crystal decided to be helpful. Once more, it glowed in my hands. The princess and I sat back on the floor with the others. With a flash of red light, a scene unfolded. We could see a wall with a tapestry depicting a knight on horseback fighting a three-headed dragon.

"Three heads, pah! That's nothing," said Jezebel.

"Shh!" I said.

The tapestry seemed to float away from the wall as if disturbed by a breeze. Behind it was a hidden door, and beyond the door, a winding stairway leading up. The scene in the crystal moved, floating up the stairway, around and around. A window revealed the countryside spreading out far below: rolling hills, trees, streams, and mountains. The hidden stairway was obviously high up in one of the castle turrets. At the top of the stairs was a landing and a single door. We passed through the heavy wooden door like ghosts and into a small, circular room, with a bit of odd furniture, a few chairs, an old desk. At the far end, I could see my dad. He was unconscious and locked in a cell. On his wrists were manacles that glowed faintly with magic— probably to keep him from using a spell to escape. The scene grew hazy, then the crystal went dark.

"Okay, I have a plan," said Ileana. "I'll go after the dragons and meet you at that window we saw. You three get Master Dreadthorn out."

"How do we know you won't just betray us to the heroes?" asked Jezebel.

"Why would I do that?" Ileana asked.

"Oh, I don't know, maybe because it's your destiny!" Jezebel said. "Maybe you want to win Rune's power!"

"Rune doesn't have any power!" Ileana said.

"Hey!" I said.

"We're wasting time. I'm going." The princess stood up, dusted off her hero costume, and held out her hand to me. I thought she was trying to help me up, but then she frowned when I took her hand.

"No, Rune," she said. "I need the crystal."

"What for?" I asked, wondering if I would ever be able to trust Ileana again.

"Uh, to keep it safe from Deven. To find the right tower when I come to rescue you."

"I think you'll be able to find it without the crystal," I said, hugging the crystal ball tighter to my chest. "It'll be the one with a bunch of villains hanging out of it."

"Exactly," said Ileana. "You guys are going to be running from Deven. You don't want him to get the crystal back. It'll be safe with me."

"Until you betray us!" said Jezebel.

"For the last time, I'm not going to betray anybody!" Ileana said. "Although I'm seriously thinking about hexing *you*, Countess!"

"Don't threaten Jezebel!" I said.

The look on Ileana's face was almost enough to make me feel guilty. Almost. But I couldn't help thinking about the prophecy and all the secrets that surrounded us. What if Ileana was trying to steal some kind of power from me? I mean, sure, she was my sister, but how well did I really know her, anyway?

"Keep the dumb thing! I don't even want it!" Ileana shouted as she made her way to the bathroom stall with the sewage grate.

"Where are you going?" asked Wolf. Ileana was sliding the grate away from the hole.

"Where I said I was going. To get the dragons. You'd better be ready, or I might just leave you all here!" she said, then disappeared beneath the floor.

"Don't forget our clothes!" Wolf said. I don't know if Ileana heard him or not. Or if she cared.

I stared at the empty stall, and for a second I thought about going after her, but I didn't.

"Come on," I said after Ileana was gone. "We have to find that tapestry."

We opened the bathroom door to find Invis-a-boy still keeping watch.

"Where's the princess?" he asked.

"She had to go find our ride out of here," I said. "She'll be back, though. I hope. Anyway, can you help us find something? We're looking for a tapestry of a knight fighting a three-headed dragon."

Invis-a-boy nodded and said, "Follow me."

Jez, Wolf, and I followed him down the hallways, which were mostly empty now, as the heroes had presumably all gone to class. I wondered if anybody was still searching for us, but I didn't have long to wonder.

"There they are!" someone yelled.

We whipped our heads around. At the far end of the hallway stood Deven Do-Good, Omnibrain, Vortex, and someone who looked like a pink hippo. It was the Queen Bee. She was so swollen with bee stings she looked like a fleshy pink water balloon about to pop.

"Get them!" she shouted. Only her lips were all swollen, so it sounded more like "Guh-uhm!"

The young heroes raced up the hall toward us. Jez popped into a bat and ducked into my cape just as Vortex sent a whirlwind down the hall, lifting up all the curtains and letting in deadly sunlight.

We turned to run, but I realized Invis-a-boy wasn't following.

"Come on!" I shouted.

"Go!" he said. "Down this hall, take two lefts, then down the stairs to the right you'll find the tapestry!"

"What about you?" asked Wolf.

"I'll hold them off!" he said.

"Are you mental?" I asked, knowing the scrawny little kid didn't stand a chance against even one of the heroes, let alone all of them together.

"Just go! Rescue your father! And tell the princess not to forget me!" Then, with a high-pitched yell, he charged down the hall toward Deven's gang.

"*Heroes*," I muttered as Wolf and I fled in the other direction with Jezebel tucked safely in my cape.

We rounded the first corner, and I heard screams coming from behind us. Wolf and I ignored the sounds and kept running. We dashed around another corner, then descended a short flight of stairs. To the right was a hallway. We ran in that direction and searched the walls.

"Here!" Wolf shouted.

We stopped in front of the tapestry of the knight and the dragon. Behind us I could hear the heroes closing in. Invis-a-boy had managed to stall them, but now the chase was back on. I yanked the tapestry aside and cried out in surprise.

"Where's the door?" Wolf asked.

The crystal had clearly shown a doorway behind the tapestry, but we were looking at a solid stone wall. No door.

"Maybe it's the wrong tapestry?" Wolf offered.

I let the tapestry fall back into place and examined it. I even counted the dragon's heads to be sure. Three, just like in the crystal. This was the right tapestry.

"I don't understand," I said.

"The crystal was wrong," said Wolf.

At the far end of the hall, I could see the heroes coming down the stairway. We had to hide. I grabbed Wolf by his tail and yanked him behind the tapestry.

"This is the dumbest hiding place in the history of forever," he said. "Only an idiot wouldn't notice us hiding here."

"Do you have a better idea?" I asked.

But Wolf didn't get a chance to answer. As soon as we pressed our backs against the wall, it swung open, revealing a hidden door. We fell backward into the wall, and it closed up again.

Wolf and I found ourselves in the turret stairway,

just as the crystal had shown us. I looked back at the door and saw the hidden mechanism that allowed it to open. It had probably been triggered by us pressing some kind of secret lever in the wall.

"What's going on?" Jezebel asked, poking her bat noggin out from under my cape.

"Nope," I said, pressing her back in. "There's a window in here."

"What are you doing, Rune?" Wolf asked. I was pulling at a loose stone in the wall. It came out, tumbling to the floor.

"This," I said, shoving the broken stone under the mechanism, so the door wouldn't open. "It should buy us some time. Come on!"

We raced up the winding stairs, past the window. I glanced briefly outside, scanning the skies for Ileana and the dragons. I didn't see them. I tried not to let myself panic, not to let myself believe that she would betray us. Instead I focused on finding my dad.

At the top of the stairs was the little landing and the door. We pushed our way in and found the cell with my dad. He was no longer unconscious, but he was still wearing the magical handcuffs on his wrists.

"It's about time," was all he said. No *thank you*. No signs of worrying for his son's safety. "What *are* you wearing?"

I glanced down at my superhero costume and

blushed. Then I noticed my dad wasn't alone in the cell.

"Who's that?" I asked.

"Who?" Jezebel asked, venturing another peek from beneath my cape. When she saw the room was windowless, she flew out and transformed back into a girl.

"I would venture to guess it is the Master of this school, Doctor Do-Good," Master Dreadthorn said in his bored voice.

Upon closer inspection, I could see it *was* the doctor. He was slumped over, and obviously unconscious.

Just then, we heard something that sounded like a raging tornado from somewhere below us.

"It must be Vortex! They're trying to break through the door!" I said.

"How do we get Master Dreadthorn out?" Wolf asked.

"I don't know. I guess I'll have to use a spell," I said uncertainly. I wasn't exactly the best Speller. Sometimes accidents happened, usually involving setting people's pants on fire.

"Or you could spare me bodily injury and use the keys," the Dread Master said, nodding toward the wall where the keys were hanging.

"Right," I said, yanking the keys from their hook and unlocking the cell.

"Where are the keys for the handcuffs?" I asked.

"If I had them," said Master Dreadthorn, "I wouldn't need you."

"Right," I said again. "We'll have to get them off later."

Another explosion sounded from below. I could hear shouting. It wouldn't be long before the heroes broke through.

"So, what's the plan, Rune?" Jezebel asked. "You got us up here, now how are we getting out? Do you expect us to just fly out the window?"

"Yes," I said, opening the door and running back into the stairway. Jezebel squeaked in surprise and popped back into a bat. This time, she had to hide in Wolf's cape since I was standing in full sunlight.

"Do you see her?" Wolf asked.

"See who?" asked Master Dreadthorn.

"Ileana," said Wolf.

"No," I answered with disappointment.

I mean, I knew the prophecy had pretty much predicted it, but I just couldn't believe after all we'd been through together that Ileana would betray me.

"Now what?" asked Wolf as I came back into the room. Below us, at the bottom of the winding staircase, I heard a loud crashing sound.

I shut the door and braced it with a chair.

"Good work, Rune," said Master Dreadthorn. "First *I* was imprisoned, now we all are. Bravo."

We heard feet pounding up the stairs, and with one gust, Vortex sent the door flying from its hinges, nearly slicing off my head.

When the swirling debris settled, Deven, Vortex, and Omnibrain were all standing between us and escape. We were trapped. I didn't see the Queen Bee anywhere. I assumed she and Invis-a-boy were still hashing it out somewhere in the corridors.

"Really, Rune? You came here just to save your dad?" Deven asked as the three heroes moved slowly into the room. "Why? All he does is humiliate you, betray you, and lie to you."

"He's got a point," Wolf said. The Dread Master's cold eyes fell on him. "Sorry," Wolf added quickly.

"I do what is necessary to teach him. That is all," said Master Dreadthorn.

"Does that include lying to him about his mother? His sister?" Deven asked with a smirk. "Oh, yes. I know. Morgana told me everything."

"I don't answer to you," Master Dreadthorn said, his eyes boring into Deven Do-Good.

I was starting to wonder if Deven had a point. I mean, my dad had been a jerk to me all my life. He'd taken me away from my mother, lied to me. But then he kind of had to. I mean, the crystal had revealed that my mother couldn't keep me. What was my dad supposed to do?

I didn't have time to sort out all the drama. We came to get my dad and reclaim the villain school from Morgana. That was all I cared about right now.

"Face it, you've lost," Deven said. "No one can save you now."

We heard a terrible ripping sound and a loud roar. The ceiling tore away, and bright sunlight streamed in. Lucky for Jezebel, she was still hidden in Wolf's cape. Above us, Custard roared and dipped, flapping her golden wings in the air. Beside her, Fafnir wheezed and flew kind of lazily with Ileana perched on his scaly back.

Before anyone could react, Custard dived into the room. Her immense body was too much for the little space. The young dragon's tail thrashed, knocking over furniture and slicing through the cell bars like they were made of butter. In seconds, the room was demolished.

The heroes had taken refuge under the tattered remains of an old wooden desk. Deven peered out. We locked eyes just as one of Custard's taloned claws wrapped around me, plucking me from the tower room. Beside me, in her other claw, was Wolf. We were lifted up just as Fafnir dived into the room to rescue my dad.

"This isn't over, Rune Drexler!" Deven shouted after us.

Briefly, I wondered if he would come after us. After all, he could fly, but he didn't follow. I figured Deven wouldn't fight alone against two dragons. No, he would get some help, then come after us. In seconds, we were airborne, and Doctor Do-Good's School for Superior Superheroes was shrinking behind us.

CHAPTER FOURTEEN

Back to School

We flew on for a while longer, just to be sure no one was following us, then the dragons landed in a clearing. That was when I realized we'd picked up some extra baggage.

"What's *he* doing here?" I shouted, tumbling out of Custard's claws and over to where Fafnir had landed with Ileana, my dad—and a still-unconscious Doctor Do-Good.

"Oh, you're welcome," Ileana said, sliding down from the old dragon's back. "No, it was no trouble at all. I was happy to save you after you accused me of betraying you." She crossed her arms and thumped her foot. She had changed back into her dress.

"Do you have our clothes, too?" Wolf asked hopefully.

"I might," Ileana said, "and I might not. I think all of you have something to say to me first."

"Sorry!" Wolf said, holding out his hand for his clothes.

Ileana raised her eyebrows at me. I took a deep breath.

"I'm sorry," I mumbled.

"What was that?" Ileana asked, cupping her hand to her ear.

"I'm sorry I thought you would betray us to the heroes," I said loudly.

"Now can I have my clothes?" Wolf asked eagerly. I knew he was ready to be rid of the hateful cape, but Jez was still hiding from the fading sunlight.

"Not yet," said Ileana. "There's someone else who needs to apologize." She looked meaningfully at Wolf's cape.

"Not a chance," came Jezebel's squeaky bat voice. "You could still betray Rune!"

"C'mon, Jez!" said Wolf. "If you don't apologize, I'll have to stay in this outfit forever!"

"Don't be dense," Jez squeaked. "You can change when we get back."

"Yeah," I added, "but that means we'll have to enter the school dressed as superheroes. Including you, Jezebel."

"I'll just stay a bat then," she said.

"Okay, but you're not hiding in our capes. I hope you like the sunlight," I said, reaching in to grab her. She squeaked frantically beneath Wolf's cape.

"Fine! Sorry," Jez said, finally.

Ileana nodded and smiled and gave us all our clothes. We took turns changing behind a tree. Wolf transferred Jez from his cape to my cloak. After the sun finally set, Jez turned back into a girl and changed, too.

When we were done, we gathered around Doctor Do-Good, who was completely zonked. A thin string of drool ran down his chin like a trail of slug slime. Beside him, my dad held out his shackled hands to Ileana.

"Do you mind?" he asked. She looked at him.

"Why didn't you tell us that we were twins?" she asked.

My dad stared for a moment, then sighed.

"Obviously a conversation needs to take place. But now is not the time, Princess," he said, still holding out his hands.

"When is the time, then?" Ileana asked. "When is the time to tell somebody you're her father?"

I could see Ileana's eyes filling up with tears. Wolf coughed uncomfortably, and Jezebel grabbed his furry arm and led him off to the other side of the clearing. I just poked my foot in the grass and tried to look everywhere but at the princess. Did I mention villains aren't good with emotions?

"A good time might be when we are back at villain school," said my dad, boring into Ileana with his shark-like eyes. "Right now, I'm guessing that an entire army of superheroes is about to descend on my students in search of him." My dad poked Doctor Do-Good with his boot. "I'm also guessing that since you were all able to escape Morgana's clutches, you most likely had help from Queen Catalina, which means she might be in danger. Where exactly did you leave her when the four of you went truant?"

Ileana and I exchanged a guilty glance.

"She was safe," I said. "I mean, she should've been. Right?" I asked. "Unless—unless Morgana found her before the spell wore off or something."

"Spell?" asked Master Dreadthorn. He turned his eyes on me. "You hexed your own mother?" My eyes got big and I shook my head and pointed my finger at Ileana. Hey, no loyalty among villains.

"Well done, Ileana!" my dad said.

"What?" I asked in disbelief.

His mouth twitched in a funny kind of way, and I realized he was smiling. "It's not easy to catch Cat, uh, *Catalina* off her guard."

Oh sure. I braved a school full of superheroes to

rescue him, and not even a thank-you, but Ileana hexed our mom, and it's "Well done, Ileana!"

Ileana smiled at our dad, then her face fell.

"You're right, Rune," she said.

"I am?"

"About Mother. We didn't exactly sneak quietly out of the school when we left."

I recalled how we blasted our way through the walls of the dragons' cavern. Someone would've come to investigate. Would the spell have worn off by then? Or would the queen have stood helplessly as Morgana descended on her? Ileana seemed to be thinking the same thing.

"We have to get back," said the princess. She sucked in a deep breath, pulled out one of her hairpins, and tried to pick my dad's lock.

Ileana was the best lock-pick I'd ever seen, so when a few minutes had gone by, and my dad was still in chains, I began to worry.

"I don't understand," Ileana said with frustration. "I've never seen a lock like this."

"It's magical," I said, "maybe it can't be picked."

"I've picked magical locks before," said the princess, biting down on her tongue and working feverishly.

"These must be different," I said when her hairpin broke, and my dad remained handcuffed.

"My mom could do it," Ileana said, remounting Fafnir. "Come on. Once we get back to the school, she'll set you free."

I expected my dad to berate the princess for failing, but he didn't. Boy, I could already see who the favorite child was. In a few minutes, we were all mounted on the dragons. Doctor Do-Good was still unconscious on the ground.

"What do we do with him? Leave him here?" I asked.

"No," my dad said. "Bring him along. We might need him."

"For what? Weapons practice?" I asked. My dad glared at me.

"You heard the man," I said to the dragons. "Bring him along."

Ileana passed the message to Custard, who scooped up Doctor Do-Good in her talons.

The sky was a deep purple when we arrived at the entrance to the school. Ileana commanded the dragons to roam freely but not to go too far from the school, then she used a spell to make Doctor Do-Good float along beside as I led the way through the castle ruins toward the front entrance.

"Not that way," my dad said. "Morgana might have it guarded."

"What other way is there? Back through the hole we made in the dragons' cavern?"

"No, there is another way," Master Dreadthorn said. Then he did his slow, creepy turntable spin, raising his hands to his face, his fingers steepled. "But you must never reveal it to another living being on penalty of *death*."

We all exchanged nervous glances and followed my dad to a nearby hill as night descended. With the cool of the evening, an eerie fog crept into the low places. As we crested the hill, I realized where we were going and shuddered.

Mist ghosted across the grass so that only the tallest tombs could be seen. They floated in the fog like lost ships. Gnarled trees twisted their ancient branches toward the smile of a crescent moon that made the mist glow. Being a villain, I might be expected to gravitate to a place like this, but I couldn't help feeling a chill as we passed through the iron gate of Silent Hill Cemetery.

CHAPTER FIFTEEN

A Grave Situation

We wound our way through the maze of tombs as the night grew colder. Every cracking branch and rustling leaf made us jump.

"What about ghosts?" Wolf whispered behind me, his tail drooping as his eyes darted from side to side.

"There's no such thing as ghosts," said Jezebel.

"Says a vampire," added Ileana.

"Rune," Wolf whispered, moving closer to me.

"What?"

"You don't think your dad's going to bury us in shallow graves, do you?"

"Nah," I said. "He's very thorough. I'm sure they'll be a proper six feet under."

Wolf's eyes got huge, so I smiled reassuringly and patted his hairy back.

"We just saved him, Wolf. He's not going to do any-thing to us." I hoped.

"Be silent," my dad said.

"As the grave," I added with a chuckle. This earned me an evil glare.

"In here," he said, stopping in front of a stone build-ing. It was a mausoleum—a crypt. I really didn't want to find out what was inside, but it looked like my options were pretty slim.

Wolf gave me a meaningful look and whimpered.

"Why in here?" I asked.

"Because I said so."

We followed my dad into the tomb. Once we were all crammed inside, Master Dreadthorn reached up, took a torch from the wall, and handed it to me.

"Well?" he asked.

"What?"

"Light it, Rune."

"Oh! Right." After singeing Wolf's fur and burn-ing a hole in the Dread Master's cloak, I finally man-aged it.

The sudden glow of light revealed a small, square room of stone. It smelled damp, and I could see moss growing in the cracks in the wall. In the middle of the crypt was a long, rectangular box. I really didn't want to know what was in it, but I had no choice because my dad reached for an old vase on a shelf. The vase must have been some kind of lever, because gears grinded and the lid on the coffin slid slowly open.

Beside me, Wolf whimpered again, and his tail drooped even more. Ileana moved away from the casket, and even Jezebel looked worried. I held up the torch, expecting to see old dry bones and shreds of ancient cloth. Instead, I was looking at a staircase that descended down inside the coffin.

"A secret passage!" said Jezebel.

"And it will remain a secret unless the four of you want to spend the remainder of your educations dangling over boiling cauldrons. Understood?"

We quickly nodded in agreement.

My dad took the torch from me and disappeared into the coffin. Jez went next, then Wolf, then Ileana with the still-unconscious Doctor Do-Good floating beside her. I brought up the rear. My dad pulled a lever at the bottom of the staircase, and the lid of the casket ground back into place, leaving us in darkness.

We walked along an old tunnel that felt very similar to our school passageways, only a bit darker and moldier. Every once in a while, water would drip into some unseen puddle with a tiny *plop*. Other than that, the crackling of the torch and the soft thud of our own footsteps were the only sounds.

The tunnel ended suddenly in a flat stone wall. My dad handed the torch to Jezebel and motioned for us to be quiet. He reached up with his bound hands, slid aside a small panel on the wall, and pressed his face to it.

Master Dreadthorn gasped suddenly, then spun around, pointed at me, and wiggled one of his pale fingers, motioning for me to come look. I padded across the floor and raised my eyes to the peephole. It took me a minute to understand what I was seeing. It was a room, obviously. There was a door on the far side, opposite me. Closer was a desk. A black onyx desk. I was looking at the Dread Master's study. And a moment later, I realized something else. I was looking at his study through his glass cabinet, the one where he kept his precious crystal locked up. The crystal that was currently tucked away in my cloak.

Directly in front of me, I could make out the back of a blond head. Morgana was sitting at the Dread Master's desk. And beyond the desk a woman stepped into view. Her hands were bound with magical manacles. It was Queen Catalina. No, this wasn't just the kindly queen, this was my *mother*. An angry shock went through me at seeing her handcuffed like that.

"You can't keep me locked up here forever, Morgana. It's only a matter of time before Veldin comes to reclaim his school," said the queen. "You should run while you still can."

Morgana laughed.

"Oh, Cat. Still haven't figured out how to be a villain. Let me give you a few tips. First, villains don't come to the rescue. We undermine. We scheme. That's what I do. That's what Veldin does."

"You're wrong. He'll come here, and he'll save me, and you'll be sorry."

"Maybe the old Veldin would have. But when you left, he changed, Cat. He's not the man you once loved. Now he's as ruthless as any villain. Well, except me, of course. Really, you leaving was probably the best thing that ever happened to him. There's no love in him now."

"That's not true!" said the queen. "He loves his children. And they're going to rescue him."

More laughter.

"I think not. An entire school of superheroes against four wayward villains? They're probably locked in a tower room as we speak. In fact, with any luck, they're already— What was that?"

The ground shook. I backed away from the spy hole. For a moment, nothing happened, then the ground shook again, louder this time. Dust and dirt rained down from overhead as the shuddering continued.

We stepped back from the wall. My dad looked meaningfully at the floating Doctor Do-Good.

"The heroes have come," he said.

We heard shouting, and I raised my eyes to the spy hole again.

A man had burst into the room, one of Morgana's guards.

"Mistress! The school is under attack!" he said.

"Attack? From whom?" she asked.

"Superheroes!"

"What!" said Morgana. "Why that little two-timing weasel Do-Good! He'll be sorry he ever crossed Mistress Morgana! Gather the school Masters and all the Apprentices. Assemble them at the front entrance! Now!"

"Right away, Mistress," the man said, then dashed out the door.

"Cat, sorry we couldn't chat longer, but duty calls. Being the Mistress of two schools is *such* a burden. Why don't you just sit a spell?"

With that, Morgana hexed the queen, causing her to sink into a chair, where she was unable to move.

"Let me out, Morgana. I can help you!"

Morgana laughed bitterly.

"Oh, Cat. Do you really think I'd let you go? No, I have other plans for you. Once I chase off this rabble of superheroes, I think I'll set my sights on your kingdom next. I believe I'd look rather fetching in a crown, don't you? Ta!"

Morgana stopped to check herself in a mirror, then left the room.

"Morgana's gone," I said. "Can you believe her?"

"Yeah," said Ileana. "And I thought Jezebel was conceited."

Jez hissed at the princess.

"What now?" asked Wolf.

"Step away," said my dad.

Then he reached into his shirt pocket and pulled out the chain of keys he kept around his neck. He found the one he was looking for.

"That stone, Rune. Move it." He pointed to a small round stone in the wall.

I reached up and pushed on it. The stone slid aside, revealing a keyhole. My dad took the key in both hands, fit it into the keyhole, then turned. With a click, the wall vibrated, then slid open, and we stepped into the study.

"It's about time!" said the queen with a huge smile on her face.

CHAPTER SIXTEEN

What's Bugging Doctor Do-Good

Mom!" Ileana said, bounding across the room and embracing her mother.

"Would you be a dear and get me out of this chair?" asked Queen Catalina.

It only took Ileana two tries to find the right spell to free the queen.

"And how about these?" asked the queen, holding up her magical manacles.

"Um. I haven't had the best luck with this style of handcuffs, but I'll lend you my last hairpin," said Ileana.

The queen worked to free her own wrists. Then my dad held up his.

"If you don't mind," he said.

"You couldn't unlock them?" the queen asked Ileana.

175

Ileana crossed her arms and pouted her lips. "No."

"Here, let me show you the trick." The princess watched as her mother worked at the Dread Master's chains.

"See?" asked the queen. "If you bend it this way and then turn it just a half turn."

"Oh! I see!" said Ileana, taking over the job from her mother. A moment later, there was a tiny click, and my dad was free.

"And who is this?" asked the queen, pointing at the floating doctor.

"Long story," I said.

"And there's no time to tell it. Right now we have to fight off the superheroes and rid ourselves of Morgana," said my dad.

"Right!" I said. "Let's go!"

"Rune," said my dad, holding out his hand.

I just looked at it. Was I supposed to shake it? Slap it? High-five? What? He seemed to notice my confusion.

"The crystal, Rune."

"Oh."

I reached into my cloak and fished out the crystal ball, handing it to my dad.

"Show us why the heroes attack us," he commanded.

We all gathered around the crystal, where a scene unfolded. It showed Deven Do-Good rallying the super-heroes.

"My fellow heroes!" said Deven. "The villain prisoner has escaped along with the other villains! But I have even graver news! They've taken our beloved mentor, my father, Doctor Do-Good, as a hostage! We must go to their cursed school and fight them! You followed my father. Now follow me to his rescue and to victory!"

There was a loud cheer from the assembled teachers and students of Doctor Do-Good's school.

"Gather out front! We'll leave immediately!" said Deven.

As the crowds were dispersing, he turned to his cronies Omnibrain, Vortex, and Aero-boy.

"We have to get to my father before anyone else does," he said. "If he wakes up, he'll tell the heroes about our plan to take over this school. We'll be ruined! We have to get rid of him, and tell everyone the villains did it. Then we'll crush their school! After that, no one will question our authority!"

"I dunno, Dev," said Aero-boy. "Maybe we should just rescue your dad. If we do, he might forgive you and—"

"No! We've come too far for that!" Deven said.

"Yeah, Aero. Don't be such a baby," said Omnibrain. Aero frowned but kept silent.

"Let's go!" said Deven.

The scene in the crystal faded.

"So, now what?" asked Jezebel, hands on her hips.

She looked defiant, but I could tell Jez was nervous. Whatever Morgana's faults, she was right about one thing: *An entire school of superheroes against four wayward villains?* Even with the Dread Master and the queen thrown in, it still was not good odds.

"We have to get rid of Morgana, but we have to stop the superheroes, too!" said Ileana.

"How do we do that?" asked Wolf, nervously wringing his tail between his paws.

"Leave Morgana to me!" said Cat, her eyes flashing. I think Morgana had underestimated the queen as a villain—and an enemy.

"No," said my dad. "I'm going with you." For a brief moment, he and the queen locked eyes. Then he turned away quickly and cleared his throat.

"And what do we do?" I asked. My dad looked at the comatose Doctor Do-Good.

"Isn't it obvious, Rune?" asked my dad. "You have to protect that superhero."

"What?" My jaw dropped.

My dad sighed. "He's the only one who can expose Deven Do-Good as a traitor to the heroes. You have to find a way to wake him up before the heroes destroy this school."

With my dad and the queen gone, Jez, Wolf, Ileana,

and I were left staring at the floating form of Doctor Do-Good. Ileana released the spell, and he fell to the ground, landing on Wolf's tail.

"Aaarf!" Wolf barked in pain and surprise. He yanked his tail out from under the unconscious hero.

"Now what?" Ileana asked.

"We have to find a way to wake him up," said Jezebel.

Wolf poked him in the ribs. "Wake up!"

"Uh, Wolf," I said, "if dragons, spells, and villain abduction didn't wake him up, I don't think poking him is going to work. It's like he's under some kind of enchantment."

"No," Jez said. "Hero powers are different from villain powers. Heroes always have a weakness—one fatal flaw that drains their powers. If only we knew what Doctor Do-Good's weakness was, then we could find a way to counter it."

"Hang on a second," I said. "Remember when we were following Deven at hero school? I watched him take out a jar of something, some kind of creature, and use it to subdue his father."

"What was it?" asked Ileana.

"I couldn't see. Maybe, maybe whatever it was is still on him. Search him."

Outside the door of my dad's study, we heard a thunderous explosion and the sound of feet pounding as students and teachers rushed to defend the school against attack.

"We don't have much time. Hurry!" I said.

Everyone began to pat down the doctor, taking off his boots, searching his pockets. We couldn't find anything.

"Help me get his shirt off," I said.

"Aaaaa!" Jez shouted in alarm as Wolf and I removed Doctor Do-Good's shirt.

"What?" I asked frantically. "Did you find something?"

"No, but *cat-a-bats*, does he have a hairy back!"

"What's wrong with that?" Wolf asked with a frown.

"Awww! Look at this! It's so adorable!" said Ileana in her cutesy voice that was reserved for when she saw a baby or was holding a kitten or something gross like that.

"What now?" I asked, rolling my eyes. "Don't tell me! He has a tattoo of a baby dolphin."

"No, Rune. But he does have this little guy hitching a ride behind his ear. Look." Ileana held up her hand, where a tiny orange creature crawled lazily across her fingers.

"What is that?" asked Wolf, wrinkling his snout in disgust.

"Eww! It's a bug! Squish it!" said Jezebel, backing away.

"No! Don't hurt it. It's just an itty-bitty caterpillar," said Ileana.

Doctor Do-Good's eyes fluttered open.

"What—what's happening? Where am I?" he asked. Then he saw the caterpillar in Ileana's hand. "Get that thing away from me!" Do-Good scrambled to his feet and backed away.

We all looked confused for a moment, then I realized what had happened.

"Of course!" I said. "Deven had a jar full of caterpillars! When they touched Doctor Do-Good, his powers were drained. Caterpillars are his weakness!"

Wolf snickered. "Caterpillars are your weakness? That's just sad, man."

Doctor Do-Good reached out his hand and lifted Wolf off the ground by the scruff of his neck. "What was that, young pup?"

"Uh, nothing. Sorry, sir," Wolf said.

"Can someone please tell me what's going on?" asked the doctor, releasing Wolf. I handed him his shirt back.

"We need your help, Doctor Do-Good," I said. There was another explosion, closer this time.

"What do you mean?" he asked.

We tried to explain everything to him, how Deven had made a pact with Morgana and kidnapped my father. How he'd betrayed the doctor, his own father, and planned to take over the hero community.

"And now he's here, attacking our school. Please, won't you do something?" I asked.

"I don't know if I should," said the doctor. "After all, this is a school of villains. Maybe I should let my heroes destroy all of you."

I didn't really have an answer for that, but thankfully Jezebel did.

"Oh, we're the villains?" she asked, getting all up in the doctor's face. "*We're* the villains! Our school Master was kidnapped by *your* son. The same person who made a pact with a villain witch to deceive you. The same person who betrayed and imprisoned you, who used your one weakness against you."

"And who was it that saved you from your tower prison?" added Ileana. "Who saved you from this?" she asked, holding up the little squirmy caterpillar.

Doctor Do-Good flinched away.

"You owe us," Jezebel said.

"It seems I might have been mistaken," said Do-Good. "You're right. I will help you. This one time."

"What's the plan, Rune?" asked Wolf.

"We have to get Doctor Do-Good to explain to the

heroes that Deven is a traitor. He can convince them to stop the attack. Let's go."

"Wait," said Do-Good, reaching out his hand to stop me. "There's something you should know first, in case anything happens to me."

"What?" I asked.

"Deven's weakness. I'll tell you what it is, and you'll be able to subdue his powers."

We all exchanged glances, then I looked back at the doctor.

"Tell us."

CHAPTER SEVENTEEN

Villains Vanquished

Another explosion and more shouts echoed through the corridors. The sounds were getting much closer.

We rushed out the door into the hallway, and straight into Deven Do-Good and his gang.

"Deven!" Doctor Do-Good shouted.

"Father!" Deven looked alarmed, but quickly recovered. He rushed forward and hugged Doctor Do-Good. "Thank goodness you're safe! We've been so worried!"

"Worried?" asked the doctor. "You tried to betray me!" He pushed his son away.

"What are you talking about?" asked Deven.

"You used my weakness against me, locked me in a prison. I had to be rescued by . . . by a bunch of villains!"

"No, that's not true, Father. I would never do that.

These villains put a spell on you!" Deven pointed an accusing finger at us.

Doctor Do-Good looked at us. I could tell he was confused. Behind him Deven smiled wickedly at me.

"He's lying!" I said. "He's trying to trick you. Don't trust him."

"Oh, of course, villain. As if my own father would trust a warlock's word over his son's. Father, they came to our school and kidnapped you. Do you remember anything?"

"I—I remember you betraying me, Deven."

"Why would I do that? You had just welcomed me back after I brought you a villain Master as a prisoner, Father."

"Yes," said Doctor Do-Good, rubbing his temples. "I remember that, but . . . I just don't know what to believe."

"Then let me prove my loyalty to you, Father. Get them!" he shouted to Vortex, Aero-boy, and Omnibrain.

Vortex blasted us with a rush of swirling wind. I ducked to the right with Jezebel while Ileana shoved Wolf to the left. Immediately, Ileana shot a spell at Vortex.

While they struggled against each other, Omnibrain went after Wolf, and Aero-boy levitated toward Jezebel. I heard the tiny *pop* that meant Jez had changed into a bat, but I didn't see it happen. My focus was on Deven Do-Good.

I tried to hex him, but he flew to the side and came up behind me. I spun around, throwing another spell, but again, he was too quick.

A scream distracted me. I turned to see Wolf Junior with his head in his paws, writhing in agony. Beside him, Omnibrain had his hands to his temples and was concentrating his energy on Wolf. I realized the big-headed hero was using some kind of mind power to torture Wolf. I ran to help my ally, but before I could, someone grabbed my wrists, and I found myself chained.

When I turned around, I was surprised to see Doctor Do-Good. He had captured me. Then he chained Wolf, who, being released from Omnibrain's power, fell limply to the floor. It wasn't long before all my allies were in chains. Even Jezebel had been captured. Aero-boy was dragging her down the hall toward us.

"Good work, Father!" said Deven, patting the doctor on the back. "Why don't you take them back into the study while the boys and I rejoin the fight?"

"I'm sorry I doubted you, son," said Doctor Do-Good as he shoved Wolf, Jez, Ileana, and me into my dad's study.

"You couldn't help it. You were deceived," said

Deven, coming up behind his father. He had something in his hands.

"Doctor Do-Good! Look out!" I shouted, but I was too late. Deven had dumped the entire jar of caterpillars directly on his father's head. The old superhero collapsed to the floor, unconscious with a squirming mass of furry insects crawling all over him.

"Now I can finish you all off one by one," said Deven, bearing down on us with an evil grin, but he was interrupted by an explosion just outside the door. The fighting had finally reached us.

Out in the hallway, hexes were flying around and so were superheroes. Sparks of fire sizzled against blasts of ice as villains and heroes faced off.

"We can't let anyone see them," said Deven to his gang. "Aero-boy, you stay here and stand watch."

"But, but, Deven," said Aero-boy, frowning at the comatose Doctor Do-Good. "Doesn't this seem . . . wrong?"

"Aero," said Vortex, "why are you always such a baby?"

"I'm not a baby," Aero-boy muttered.

"Then do what Deven says, numbskull," added Omnibrain, thunking Aero-boy on his skull-cap mask.

"When the fighting is over," said Deven, "we'll come back and finish them, and tell everyone my father was destroyed in a struggle to free himself." He flashed another wicked grin at me. "But not before he took down four villain kids."

Then Deven left with Omnibrain and Vortex, closing the door behind them.

"Don't try anything funny," said Aero-boy, levitating onto my dad's desk.

"Why are you hanging out with a jerk like Deven?" asked Jezebel.

"He's not a jerk. He—he's a powerful leader," said Aero-boy, looking down at his dangling feet.

"You don't really believe that," said Ileana. "*You* could be a powerful leader, Aero-boy."

"You're trying to trick me!"

"No, I'm serious. You have a chance to do the right thing here. Doesn't he, Rune?" said the princess.

"Huh?" I asked.

Ileana raised her eyebrows meaningfully at me.

"Oh, yeah!" I said. "Why do you let Omnibrain and Vortex push you around?"

Aero-boy continued to stare at his feet. I glanced at Ileana. Behind her, Jezebel was plucking a hairpin from her head and lowering it into the princess's hands. I had to keep Aero-boy distracted.

"They totally pick on you, and Deven always takes those two guys along with him, and leaves you behind to sit and wait until the heroes get back. Aren't you sick of it?"

"But—but Deven's my friend," said Aero-boy.

"He's trying to get you in trouble. He betrayed your school Master and now he's plotting to take over the entire hero community! He's not your friend. He's a villain!" I said. It pained me to give Deven the name of *villain*, but I had no choice. I had to keep Aero-boy distracted.

The hero looked uncertainly from the unconscious Doctor Do-Good, to me, then back to the doctor again, but before he could decide what to do, Ileana was free from the handcuffs and hexing him from behind. One spell and Aero-boy was slumped over and snoring on my dad's desk.

"I did it!" Ileana said, holding up the magical manacles.

"Nice job!" Jezebel said. There was a moment of awkward silence.

"Did you actually just compliment me?" asked Ileana, breaking into a grin.

"What? It's not like I want to be Best Fiends Forever or anything," Jez said quickly. "I just meant nice job using *my* hairpin to pick the lock. That's all."

"And from behind my back, too," said Ileana. "Man, I'm *good*."

"Sadly, yes. You *are* good. Probably beyond cure," said Jezebel. "And since you obviously think you're the supreme princess of lock-picking, would you mind?" Jez held out her hands, and just like that things were back to normal between Jez and Ileana. Soon, the princess had freed all of us.

Wolf moaned in agony, clutching at his head.

"You okay?" I asked.

"Yeah, except for a raging headache. Let's go. I can't wait to get my claws into Omnibrain."

"Hang on. What about him?" I asked, pointing to the doctor.

"Forget it, Rune," said Jezebel. "He'll just betray us again."

"But how are we going to convince the heroes to stop the attack?" I asked. "We have to wake him up."

"Even if he helps us, there's no guarantee we'll be able to stop Deven," said Ileana.

"Oh, I think there is. Remember what Doctor Do-Good told us. Jezebel? Can you help?" I asked, looking meaningfully at her.

She seemed confused for a moment, then grinned wickedly. "Oh, I am *so* on it!"

With a tiny *pop* Jezebel turned into a bat and flew out of the study.

"I don't get it," said Wolf Junior. "What's going on?"

"Deven's going down. That's what's going on," I said.

We began plucking caterpillars off Doctor Do-Good. We were only about halfway finished when Aero-boy woke up.

"What are you doing to him?" he asked groggily.

Ileana prepared another hex, but I held out my hand, motioning for her to wait.

"We're saving him. He's the rightful Master of your school, not Deven. Whose side are you on, Aero-boy?"

The hero looked indecisive. Then his eyes hardened. "What do you want me to do?" he asked.

Just then Jezebel returned with a pack slung over her shoulder.

"I ran into someone in the hall," she said.

"Not Deven?"

"No, this!" Jez's fist was wrapped around a handful of nothing.

"She's finally cracked," said Ileana.

"Princess! You're safe!" squeaked a familiar voice. Slowly, Invis-a-boy materialized in his gray-and-white costume. He rushed forward to kiss Ileana's hand. Behind the tiny hero's back, Jez wrapped her hands around herself and made kissing noises. Ileana glared at her.

"We've got trouble," Jezebel said, removing her pack and tossing it to me.

"Understatement of the year," said Wolf.

"What's going on?" I asked.

"Deven and his cronies have defeated your school Masters," said Invis-a-boy.

"They've rounded up all the villain students in the cafeteria cave," added Jezebel. "I think we're too late, Rune."

"It's not over yet, but we have to hurry!" I turned to Aero-boy. "Get these caterpillars off Doctor Do-Good! When he wakes up, tell him Deven's plans. Convince him to stop this attack."

Aero-boy began frantically plucking furry insects off the doctor.

"What are you going to do?" he asked.

"We're going to stop Deven Do-Good," I said.

"How?" asked Invis-a-boy.

I reached into the bag Jezebel had brought and pulled out our secret weapon.

"With this!"

CHAPTER EIGHTEEN

Sweet Revenge

I ran toward the cafeteria cave with Wolf, Ileana, and Jezebel behind me.

When we reached the doors, we could hear Deven talking inside. I peeked through a crack and saw him standing on a lunch table with Omnibrain and Vortex beside him. The villain students were all gathered in the center of the room, and the superheroes were standing guard around them in a circle.

"I don't see Master Dreadthorn or Queen Catalina anywhere," I said. "Or Morgana. Where can they be?"

"We can't worry about that right now, Rune," said Jezebel. "We have to stop Deven before he destroys all the students!"

"Yeah, and I still need to introduce my fist to Omnibrain's face," said Wolf, pounding one furry paw into the other. Whatever Omnibrain had done to Wolf had really made him mad. He wasn't usually so, well, *tough*.

"We can't just rush in there," said Ileana. "We'll be caught before we can even reach Deven."

"She's right," added Invis-a-boy. I had a feeling the hero kid would agree with anything Ileana said.

"I might have a plan. It's dangerous, but we have to risk it," I said. "Jez, I need you to fly to Stiltskin's class-cave and get a potion bottle. Ileana, do you still have those hero costumes?"

Wolf groaned, "Not that cape again!"

After the villainesses returned, I explained the plan to my allies. When I was sure everyone understood, we put on the hero costumes.

"Everyone ready?" I asked. Wolf, Jez, and Ileana all nodded.

Together with Invis-a-boy we edged into the cafeteria cave and immediately spread out. Ileana, Wolf, Invis-a-boy, and Jezebel melted into the crowd of superheroes while I made my way to the lunch table where Deven and his cronies were standing.

"It is a sad loss," Deven was saying as I edged closer. "My father was a brave man. As he took his final breath, with his fallen foes piled at his feet, he said to me—Drexler!"

There was confused whispering from the heroes,

but Deven had spotted me. He pointed his finger and shouted.

"That's no hero! That's a villain! Get him!"

I looked left and right, where superheroes were closing in fast. Quickly, I pulled out the potion bottle, yanked the stopper, and raised it to my lips.

"Stop him! Don't let him drink that!" Deven shouted.

Before I could drink any of the potion, Omnibrain and Vortex had me in their clutches. Deven hopped down from the table. He came toward me, the crowd of heroes parting around him.

"So, you managed to escape, did you?" he asked. "And what's this, I wonder."

Deven ripped the potion bottle from my hands as I struggled against Vortex and Omnibrain.

"'Superstrength Potion'?" Deven asked, reading the label on the bottle. "Well, well, well, Drexler. Planning to be a hero, were you?"

"Don't insult me," I said. "It's heroes like you that make me proud to be called villain!" I wasn't really sure what I meant by that, but it sounded good.

Then I spat in his face. It felt pretty awesome until he punched me in the stomach. I doubled over with a groan. Finally, I managed to get a breath.

"Is that all you got?" I asked, slowly standing up again.

His face clouded in anger as he wiped the spit off his face with his sleeve.

"Guess you need to be taught a lesson, Drexler," said Deven. "Let's see how you like being punched after I drink this!"

He raised the potion bottle to his lips.

"No, don't!" I shouted, struggling even more against the iron grips of Omnibrain and Vortex.

With a wicked grin, Deven gulped down the contents of the potion bottle.

"I can feel something!" he said. Then his triumphant smile faltered. A look of dread passed over his face. Now it was my turn to smile.

"What—what's in this?" he croaked, clutching at his throat.

"Just a little hot cocoa," I said. "Courtesy of Countess Jezebel Dracula."

"No!" Deven whispered, falling to his knees. "Chocolate. Is. My. Weakness!"

Beside me, Omnibrain and Vortex had released their grips and were backing away in horror.

"Oops," I said, squatting down to where Deven was writhing on the ground. "I told you not to drink it."

A moment later, Deven had passed out.

"Now!" I shouted, and stood up.

Wolf, Jezebel, and Ileana all tore off their masks

and capes and attacked the heroes. When the other villain kids realized what was happening, they joined in the fight.

The villains were throwing hexes left and right, but we were no match against the heroes and their super-powers. It was obvious we were toast.

"Well," said Wolf Junior as Omnibrain and Vortex bore down on us, "it was a good try, Rune. There's just one more thing I have to do before we lose."

Wolf ran up to Omnibrain, who was gathering his mind power to crush us, and punched him in the nose. Wolf grinned over his shoulder at me, his dog tongue lolling, tail wagging. But his triumph was short-lived. With a blast of wind, Vortex slammed us both into the cave wall.

"You're going to regret that, dog!" Omnibrain said, clutching his nose, which was swelling almost as big as his massive cranium. He and Vortex stood over us, ready to strike, but suddenly Omnibrain fell backward. Vortex turned in confusion toward his fallen comrade, and he, too, was knocked off his feet.

"What's going on?" asked Omnibrain.

Then Vortex shot out a hand and grabbed hold of his unseen foe. There was a squeak of terror, and Invis-a-boy materialized.

"You!" shouted Vortex. "You'll pay for this!"

We were so caught up in the action that it took a second for us to realize the room had grown strangely quiet. The sounds of fighting students had died to silence.

"Stop!" said a voice just as Vortex prepared to attack Invis-a-boy.

The color drained from our attackers' faces when they saw Doctor Do-Good making his way toward us through the crowd. The other heroes all looked confused, but they did not resume their attack. The villains looked like they were going to take the opportunity to strike, but I knew I couldn't let them. If we continued to attack his students, Doctor Do-Good might decide to annihilate us after all.

"Villains, stop!" I said, scrambling to my feet. To my total amazement, they actually listened to me, or maybe they were just too tired to put up a fight anymore.

"You've been tricked," said Doctor Do-Good to all the heroes, "by my son, Deven Do-Good, and these two!" He pointed at Omnibrain and Vortex. "I was never kidnapped by villains. It was Deven who betrayed me. The villains rescued me."

Then Omnibrain and Vortex noticed Aero-boy standing behind the doctor.

"You traitor!" said Vortex.

"I'm not the traitor," said Aero-boy. "You are!"

"I told Deven he couldn't trust a spineless nobody like you, Aero!" said Omnibrain. "How did you even get into hero school?"

The purple-and-yellow-clad Aero-boy advanced on Omnibrain.

"Oooh! I'm so scared! What are you going to do, Aero? Levitate on me?"

But Aero-boy didn't slow down. He ran straight up to Omnibrain and punched his already swollen nose.

Omnibrain staggered backward with a look of shock on his face.

"Feels good, doesn't it?" said Wolf. Aero-boy rubbed his knuckles and smiled.

Vortex took one look at Omnibrain. The air began to swirl. I could tell they were going to run.

"Get the traitors!" said Doctor Do-Good.

The heroes all shouted and ran toward Vortex and Omnibrain. On the floor, Deven Do-Good was regaining consciousness.

"Father," he said weakly. "Don't let the villains trick you again."

"No, Deven. I won't be tricked again," said Do-Good. Then he locked his son in yet another set of magical manacles. I was beginning to wonder where the heroes got their supply of those things. "You're grounded, young man. A long stay in the tower would do you good."

"But, Dad!" said Deven.

"No games. No friends. And no flying."

"Awww!" Deven whined as his dad hoisted him up.

Jezebel and Ileana joined us. Wolf was already tearing off the hateful hero costume.

"If there's anything I can do to repay you—" said Do-Good.

"Actually," I said, "there might be one more thing you could help us with. Can we borrow Invis-a-boy?"

CHAPTER NINETEEN

Auntie Morgana

We'd been running around the school for what seemed like a lifetime trying to find my dad and the queen and Morgana. There was no sign of them anywhere.

Invis-a-boy was with us. Doctor Do-Good had taken Deven and the other heroes back to their school, but he'd agreed to leave Invis-a-boy behind out of gratitude, to repay their debt, blah, blah—some noble nonsense like that. The point was, a superhero was helping us, and that's what mattered.

"Where could they be?" asked Jezebel.

"If only we still had the crystal ball," I said.

"We might have something better," said the princess. Flying down the hall toward us was Tabs.

"What? Hairballs?" I asked as my father's pet cat-a-bat landed in Ileana's arms.

The princess cooed and purred at the flying cat. Jezebel rolled her eyes.

"We seriously don't have time for this," said Jez.

"Shh," Ileana said. "She's telling me something."

"Let me guess," Jez said. "She could really go for a ball of yarn and some liver treats."

"No, Countess. She said that Morgana has our parents trapped in a secret cavern just beyond the dragons' cave. Let's go."

"Impressive, Princess!" said Invis-a-boy. Jezebel hissed at him, and he grew slightly see-through and said no more.

We took the shortcut behind the Great Clock, down to the Prophecy Cave. That was a bad idea because it reminded me and Ileana that we were possibly doomed to betray each other.

"What do these words mean?" asked Invis-a-boy as we reached the Prophecy door.

Ileana and I looked at each other.

"Nothing," we said in unison.

I tugged at the door, but the old rusty hinges were making it almost impossible to open.

"Allow me," said Invis-a-boy, who helped me pull the door open. The scrawny kid was stronger than he looked.

"Uh. Thanks," I said. Most of the superheroes we'd met were stuck-up jerks, but Invis-a-boy wasn't so bad.

We made our way down into the dragons' cavern. Of course, it was empty. The dragons were still roaming around outside somewhere. Far above, I could see the gaping hole we'd made during our escape.

"So, where's this secret cavern?" asked Jezebel.

Ileana and Tabs exchanged another round of purring and cooing.

"This way," said the princess.

We followed her to the far end of the cave and a dead end.

"Well, this is what happens when you get directions from a cat," said Wolf.

"It's a *secret* cavern," said Ileana. "The entrance is hidden."

She purred to Tabs once more, then ran her hand along the rough cave wall, pressing on a section of stone that looked no different from the rest. When she touched it, I heard the rumble of machinery. Cracks appeared, and an entire section of the cave swung open like a door.

"How many secret passages *are* there in this school?" asked Wolf as we walked cautiously through the doorway. Ileana purred to the cat-a-bat.

"Tabs says there are at least eight more we don't know about," said the princess.

"Know-it-all," Wolf muttered to Tabs, sticking his doggy tongue out at her.

I found a torch on the wall, and decided to let Jezebel light it since I wasn't so good with spells involving fire. We walked down a long corridor at the end of which was a door. Even from where we were standing, I could hear muffled voices. I motioned for everyone to be quiet as we approached. In the glow of the torchlight, I saw a keyhole in the door and, handing the torch to Wolf, I bent down to peer inside.

"Well," said Morgana. "I haven't heard any explosions in a while. Perhaps the fighting is finally over. I wonder which side won. Not that it matters. Either way, I'll be in control again soon."

Morgana held up her hand. Her fingernails curled around my dad's crystal ball.

Through the keyhole, I could see Master Dreadthorn and Queen Catalina bound and hanging high in the air over a deep hole. They'd been tied together so that if Queen Cat picked the lock, the tension on the chains would release, causing them both to fall into the pit.

"You won't get away with this, Morgana," said the queen. "No matter who wins, you'll still be everyone's enemy."

"Not true," Morgana said. "If the villains win, you two will never be found. I will still be the Mistress of this school."

"And if the heroes win?" asked the queen.

"If the heroes win, I'll deliver two villain prisoners to them. They'll welcome me with open arms," said Morgana. "Then I'll graciously offer to rebuild this school for justice, honor, blah, blah, blah. I'll secretly create my own villain army right under their superhero noses. And when the time is right, I'll attack the hero school and gain even more power! Mistress Morgana's School for Superior Supervillains!"

Ugh, monologues. It was hard to believe Morgana had become such a powerful villainess when she was always blabbing her plans to everyone. I'd heard enough. I was backing away from the keyhole when Morgana said something that brought me back.

"So now the prophecy will finally be fulfilled."

Ileana and I exchanged frowns. What was Morgana talking about? I put my eye to the keyhole once more as we all gathered closer to listen.

"*In this place, inside these halls, a terrible betrayal falls* . . . Remember, Veldin?" asked Morgana. "After all these years, I've finally done it."

At this point, we were all gathered around the door with our ears pressed to it like suction cups. Of course, Jezebel chose that moment to sneeze. She staggered backward and stepped on Wolf's tail. Wolf howled, jerked his tail away, and tripped over Ileana. The princess went sprawling and landed on me. The whole fiasco ended with my face smashing into the door handle and all four of us villain kids tumbling into the secret room.

We were too surprised to put up much of a fight. If it had just been Morgana, we might have gotten the upper hand, but her two burly headsmen had been flanking the door. Before we could even think of a spell, Morgana's thugs had us chained back to back in a corner. Except for Princess Ileana. I guess Morgana caught on to her hairpin trick, because the princess was chained to the wall on the other side of the cave, far away from the rest of us. I didn't see Invis-a-boy anywhere. I know. Funny.

Maybe he'd escaped. Or maybe he'd decided villains weren't worth the trouble and gone back to his own school. Either way, this was pretty much the saddest rescue attempt in history. Morgana prowled around us like a cat and gloated. Across the room, my parents still dangled over the hole, which was some kind of old well. The cover for it was lying to one side.

"As I was saying, Veldin, before we were so rudely interrupted by your offspring, the prophecy is finally fulfilled. I've betrayed you, taken your power over the little villain minds, and now you will yield to me. I win."

"Wait," I said. "What does any of this have to do with the prophecy? It's about twins."

Morgana laughed, tossing her blond head back. I caught the sickening scent of her perfume and nearly gagged. Beside me Jezebel jerked suddenly.

"What's wrong?" asked Wolf.

"I don't know," said Jezebel. "I thought I felt something on my head." She bent forward. "Do I have a bug in my hair?"

Morgana didn't seem to notice that Jez and Wolf were talking. Instead, she went on with her embarrassing villain monologue.

"Oh, Rune, Rune, Rune. So many things you don't know. Well, I'm about to fulfill another part of the prophecy. A long-kept secret shall be revealed. Your father and I are twins. Full-villain twins, actually."

"What?" Ileana and I both said. I was related to Morgana? Blond, stinky dragon-nails Morgana? Eww.

"Yes," Morgana said. "It seems twins run in the family." She looked back and forth meaningfully between Ileana and me.

"At first, when our little band of allies discovered the prophecy all those years ago, Veldin and I worried that it might be about us. We thought if anybody else discovered the words on the wall, they might use the prophecy against us, to steal our power. So, we pretended not to be brother and sister. As the years went by, fewer and fewer people in the villain community even knew we were related, let alone full-villain twins. And my dear brother and I made a pact: that we would never try to steal each other's power. Was I convincing enough, Veldin? Did you really believe I would be content without your power?" Morgana held up the crystal ball as evidence of her victory.

"What about the rest of the prophecy, Morgana?" asked my dad.

"Yes," said Queen Catalina, "it says the traitor twin shall be betrayed."

"Veldin is the traitor!" Morgana shouted. "A traitor to his profession, with his soft-hearted ways, coddling these wayward villain children. Under my instruction they will become powerfully evil and loyal only to me!"

Wow. If the Dread Master was considered soft-hearted, I really didn't want to know what strict teaching looked like.

It was about this time that I noticed Ileana had her tongue between her teeth, the way she always did when she was concentrating hard. And she was doing something behind her back. Then I heard a voice in my ear and nearly jumped.

"It's me," whispered Invis-a-boy. "I've given the

princess the vampire girl's hairpin. We have to keep the blond witch distracted until the princess can free you."

I didn't think that would be a problem. Morgana was in a rage, telling my dad and the queen how awesome she was and how lame he was. I could see years of hidden sibling issues coming out into the open.

"To this day, Father still thinks it was me who burnt down the evil lair, Veldin! And tattling to Mother when I ran away to King Arthur's Court? You are such a mama's boy!"

Yeah. Morgana was definitely in a zone. I saw no reason to interrupt her ranting. Especially since the princess had freed herself and was quietly mumbling hexes at Morgana's beefy guards. The headsmen grew rigid with some kind of freezing spell. After dealing with the guards, the princess came up quietly and began working on the chains that held me, Wolf, and Jezebel.

We were collectively sneaking up behind Morgana, preparing to hex her, when suddenly she spun around and fired a spell. I was pulled out of the way, presumably by Invis-a-boy, but Ileana, Jez, and Wolf had been frozen by Morgana.

I fell behind an old desk, landing hard on my side and knocking my head against the floor. I had no clue where Invis-a-boy was. For all I knew, he'd been hit by

Morgana's spell and was invisibly frozen along with my other allies.

"Rune, get out of here!" Queen Catalina shouted. "Run!"

"Oh, hush!" Morgana said. The queen was silent. I assumed Morgana had hexed her, too. "He won't try that," she continued. "Will you, Rune? For a villain, he's pathetically loyal to his allies and his parents."

I could hear Morgana walking slowly toward my hiding place. Her high-heeled boots *click-click-click*ed on the cave floor. I chanced a peek around the side of the desk. A pair of the magical handcuffs was floating in midair behind Morgana's back. I knew I had to keep her distracted, and there was only one way to do that. I stood up.

"Oooh. Brave," she said with a smile. "You've been hanging around heroes too much, *nephew*."

"You're wrong, you know," I said, trying very hard not to look at the manacles that were moving silently closer to Morgana.

"Oh?" asked Morgana. She didn't even try to hex me. She was a cat, and I was a mouse to be toyed with before she ate me alive.

"The prophecy. It isn't about you and Master Dreadthorn. It's about me and Ileana."

If she could've moved, I'm sure Ileana would've given me a perplexed look. I was kind of glad my allies

210

couldn't move or react. It made it a little easier to make my bluff.

"What makes you say that?" she asked, narrowing her green eyes. I could hear a hint of doubt in her voice.

"Because Ileana has a secret power. And I've taken it from her. *We* are the twins of the prophecy."

"What are you talking about?" Morgana said. "What power?" Her voice was greedy and she stepped closer to me. Behind her, Invis-a-boy was taking his sweet time getting those handcuffs in place. I suppose he didn't want to risk making a sound, but it still felt like forever.

I could feel everybody's eyes on me: my allies, the queen, my dad. Whether they were confused or saw my plan and were giving me silent encouragement, I had no idea. It didn't matter. I had to keep talking.

"You know the words of the prophecy," I said. "*A long-kept secret is revealed.* Well, the queen was keeping Ileana's power secret. But I, uh, found out about it."

"Oh? And how did you manage that?" Morgana asked.

"I, um, read her diary," I said, which was totally true. It didn't really mention any secret power, but apparently the princess thinks this one Apprentice vampire is "totally dreamy." Her words. Not mine. What is it with girls liking vampires?

"And what was this secret power?" Morgana asked.

211

She'd made her way to the desk and was digging her nails into the wood in anticipation. The screeching noise they made was excruciating.

"Um . . ."

I was totally out of ideas. It had taken all my brain power to come up with this pretend story, and now I had nothing. Then I heard a faint clicking sound.

"That's what I thought," said Morgana, leaning forward over the desk until her face was just inches from mine. "Time to die."

Morgana raised her hands to hex me. I winced, wondering if it would hurt very much. After a few seconds, when nothing happened, I cautiously opened one of my eyes.

"What—?" Morgana looked down to see one ring of the magical manacles around her right wrist, the other ring dangling from it.

"Help!" a disembodied voice squeaked as Morgana's hand shot out into the seemingly empty air and wrapped around an invisible neck.

"Who are you?" she demanded.

With his oxygen cut off, Invis-a-boy began to appear again. As his face came into focus, Morgana squeezed harder.

This was my chance. I launched across the desk and seized the dangling chains, intent on cuffing Morgana's other wrist. She dropped Invis-a-boy, who fell to the floor coughing, and focused her hatred on me.

Red nails like razors slashed at my neck and face. And I nearly died from the wafting perfume. Still, I managed to keep hold of Morgana's cuffed wrist, while defending myself with my free hand. Behind her, Invis-a-boy got to his feet and threw all his weight on Morgana. The three of us tumbled to the cave floor. Morgana's hard leather boot struck me square in the face, then I lashed out with a wild punch, which accidentally hit Invis-a-boy in the mouth. A trickle of blood ran down his chin, but he didn't seem to notice. Instead, he threw himself on Morgana, pinning her down with her face to the floor.

"Guards! Guards!" Morgana shouted, but her headsmen were still frozen in place by Ileana's spell.

"Hurry!" Invis-a-boy yelled at me. Morgana struggled beneath us like a wild cat-a-bat.

I grappled with Morgana's other wrist, the razor claws ripping my skin. Finally, I managed to twist her arm back and click the final manacle into place. Invis-a-boy and I were out of breath and sweating like crazy, but we both managed to half smile at each other.

"Ahem," a voice said. I looked up to see the Dread Master still dangling. "Please take your time, Rune. It's so much fun hanging here."

"You're welcome," I muttered under my breath.

"What was that?" Master Dreadthorn asked sharply.

"Coming," I said.

I dragged myself to my feet and slid the cover back over the well. Once the danger of falling into the well was gone, Queen Catalina was able to pick the lock on her cuffs. My father removed the silencing spell Morgana had cast on the queen. With some more lock-picking and a few spells, Queen Catalina had everyone free. Except the guards and Morgana, of course. She was still facedown on the floor.

CHAPTER TWENTY
Evil Endings

After I'd pretty much saved the school, there were still a lot of things to do. First, we had to make sure all the students were still alive. There were a few minor injuries, but it seemed that nobody was going to croak just yet.

Next, my dad needed a suitable place to keep Morgana until Count Dracula arrived. Apparently word had finally reached him of Morgana's ambitions, and he was coming to talk with my dad and sort things out. I thoughtfully offered the Detention Dungeon as a prison for Morgana until the count's arrival.

"Now think about what you did," I said to her as she dangled upside down over a boiling cauldron, seething at us.

"This isn't over, Rune Drexler!" she said. "When I get out of here, I'm going to—"

Morgana's mouth continued to move, but no words came. Queen Catalina smiled at me and said, "When will you ever learn to stop with the monologues, Morgana?"

We left her dangling over the cauldron, shouting silently to the steamy room.

Then Invis-a-boy had to be returned to his own school. Since he couldn't fly, we lent him Fafnir to get him home.

"Are you sure about this?" he asked, eyeing the old dragon.

"Of course! Would I try to trick you?" Ileana asked, batting her royal eyelashes at Invis-a-boy and blowing him a kiss.

He gulped, smiled, stammered stupidly, and fell off Fafnir. Twice. Finally, with a rope to hang on to (and one tied around his waist just in case) we sent Invis-a-boy back to Doctor Do-Good's School for Superior Superheroes.

Just as the young hero disappeared into the evening sky, something else could be seen flying toward us.

"What's that?" asked Wolf, pointing his paw, his ears pricked alertly.

"Oh, no," said Jezebel. She hastily straightened her back and rubbed nonexistent dust from her purple dress and dark cloak. "It's my dad."

The inky form of a flying bat grew closer and closer until it was level with us. Then Dracula transformed into his not-quite-human self.

I'd seen him before, but as always, he was an imposing figure, a dark and fearful legend come to life. Imagine a really rich and powerful businessman with predator eyes, ashy skin, and pointy fangs. His clothes looked both ancient and timeless, but still flawlessly clean. His black shoes were shined to gleaming perfection. He nodded curtly to us. I couldn't help reaching up to cover my neck. Then his eyes landed on his daughter.

"Jezebel," he said.

"Father," she answered.

And that was as warm and fuzzy as things ever got in the Dracula family. He gestured for us to lead the way back into the school.

It wasn't long before we found my dad. He was in his study with Queen Catalina. Master Dreadthorn introduced her to the count, who smiled a cold, thin-lipped smile at my mother. Apparently, like his daughter, he didn't enjoy being outranked.

"Strange rumors have reached my ears, Drexler," the count said to my dad. "Heroes and traitors and all sorts of odd things. What's the truth of it?"

I expected the Dread Master to dismiss me and my

allies, but he didn't. Maybe he needed us here to give our side of the story. Or maybe we'd finally earned a little respect from the old man. But probably not.

My dad told Dracula everything, how Morgana had plotted to take over his school using Deven Do-Good to kidnap him and steal his crystal ball. This, I could see, was back in its traditional place: the glass cabinet behind my father's desk.

He told Dracula how Morgana had also imprisoned us in the Detention Dungeon and threatened us.

"Well, it sounds like Morgana showed quite a bit of initiative," Dracula said.

I wanted to scream at him. Initiative? Threatening students? Working with heroes? Stealing? Lying? Wow. She *had* shown some initiative, but I still hated her and was about to tell Dracula just what I thought. My dad seemed to sense my anger. He reached out one pale hand and held me silently back.

"But," continued the count, "I can see she is a bit *overzealous*. Perhaps she needs some time away from her duties as a villain school Mistress. Let's have a talk with her, shall we?"

My thoughts turned to Morgana's school down the coast from us. I wondered how her students had been faring without her. They probably loved it. I could picture a giant bonfire with students of all ranks dancing and shouting and tossing their berets into the flames.

My father led our party down to the Detention Dungeon. Even though it was dark and thick clouds of steam rolled in front of our eyes, we could see the room was empty. Morgana had escaped.

"Well, Veldin," said the count, "I'll take that as confirmation that Morgana wants some time off. I suppose you'll have to take over as Master of her school. Yes. Master Dreadthorn's School for Exemplary Villains. Nice ring to it, eh, Drexler? What do you say?"

"One the other's power wins," Ileana muttered beside me.

"What?" I asked. But she wasn't paying attention to me.

"Count," my father began, "I'm honored by your faith in me, but I have enough responsibility as it is looking after *these* miscreants."

He nodded toward us. I smiled at the compliment. But my dad's evil glare quickly wiped the smile from my lips.

"I wonder if you might appoint Master Stiltskin as Morgana's successor?" said Master Dreadthorn. "I'm sure he won't mind taking up the post until a suitable replacement can be found."

"If that's what you want," said Dracula with a dismissive wave of his hand. "Just send the paperwork to my secretary. And now, I'm hungry."

Wolf, Ileana, and I all covered our necks as Dracula

nodded to us and left. He never even said good-bye to Jezebel. She didn't seem to care, though. When he'd gone, she let out a sigh of relief.

"I better talk to Stiltskin," said my father. With a swirl of his cloak, he was gone.

My allies and I, along with the queen, made our way back to the upper-level caves.

"I'm starving," said Wolf. "Anyone else want to get a bite to eat?"

"Me!" said Jezebel. "You coming?" She turned to me and Ileana. The princess was looking sheepishly at her mother.

"I'd like to talk with them privately, if you don't mind," Queen Catalina said. Wolf and Jez nodded and left us alone with the queen.

"Well, it seems you had a lot of adventures after you hexed me in the dragons' caverns," said Queen Catalina.

"Why didn't you tell us?" Ileana asked. The queen's smile faded.

"We thought it would be better this way. I never expected the two of you to meet. Then, when Rune came to us on his Plot last semester, I wanted to tell you both, but Veldin asked me not to. I think, after all these years, he was still worried about the prophecy, that someone might use one or both of you, thinking you had some secret power. Or that one of you might turn against the other. You saw how Morgana reacted to it. She was so worried that her brother would steal her power, so she decided to act against him first."

Neither Ileana nor I said anything. We didn't really know what to say. The queen seemed to take our silence as anger.

"Please believe me, Rune, I would've done anything to keep you. But I knew you'd be in danger."

"I'm not mad," I said.

And I realized I wasn't. I mean, I hadn't exactly enjoyed the royal treatment like Ileana, but I'd had an okay life as a villain-in-training. If I'd been raised in some stuffy old palace, I would never have met Jezebel or Wolf.

"So what now?" asked Ileana.

"Things will go on as usual, I suppose," said the queen, wrapping one arm around each of us. "I'll return to my kingdom. You two will stay here and finish school. And maybe during summers Rune can come and spend time at the palace with us."

"Sounds good to me," I said.

"What about you and Master Dread—that is, our father?" said Ileana. "That sounds weird. I mean, I know he's my biological father, but my dad will always be, you know, the king."

"It's okay," I said to my sister. "I really don't think the Dread Master expects you to call him Dad. I don't even call him that most of the time."

"Right." Ileana turned back to our mother. "So, what about you and Master Dreadthorn?"

"The past is the past, my darling," said the queen with a sigh. "I'm married to the king now. Veldin understands that. Of course, I still care for him and wish him all the best."

After we'd talked a little longer, Queen Catalina left us. She was returning to her palace the next day. Ileana and I found Wolf and Jezebel. They'd snuck past Cook and pilfered some excellent food from the kitchen. They'd even gotten some normal food for those of us who didn't feel like chocolate bars or sheep liver. We ate in the Prophecy Cave.

"Weird, isn't it?" Jez said through a mouthful of chocolate.

"What?" I asked.

She nodded toward the cave door with her cheeks bulging. "That."

"Yeah," said Wolf, licking his lips with his doggy tongue. "It caused so much trouble, and for what? I mean, was it even true?"

"I think it was," Ileana said.

"What do you mean?" I asked.

"*In this place, inside these halls/A terrible betrayal*

falls. Well, Morgana did betray your father here," said the princess.

"Sure, but what about the rest?" asked Jez.

"*Full-villain siblings, twins/One the other's power wins,*" continued Ileana. "Morgana and Dreadthorn are full-villain twins. She took his power as school Master and eventually took his crystal ball, too."

"Go on," I said.

"*A long-kept secret is revealed/To one, the other twin must yield,*" said Ileana. "We found out their secret, the one Morgana and Dreadthorn kept for so many years . . . that they were twins. And in the end one of them would have to yield to the other by force."

"What about the last part?" asked Wolf.

"*The traitor twin shall be betrayed/And villains into heroes made,*" said Ileana. "Morgana was betrayed by Deven Do-Good when he made off with the crystal ball instead of giving it to her like she'd planned."

"And the heroes?" I asked.

"We're the heroes," Ileana said with a smile. "Whether you like it or not, we saved your dad. We saved the lives of hero and villain students. We saved Doctor Do-Good. We rescued our parents and defeated Morgana. Heroes."

"Would you keep your voice down!" I whispered.

"Okay, okay. I get it. You know, I think you're right."

I reread the lines again. It all seemed to fit. By trying

to outsmart the words of the prophecy, Morgana had actually fulfilled them and brought disaster on herself.

"Of course I'm right," said the princess.

We talked a while longer. Classes had been canceled because of all the confusion and chaos, to resume once things were cleaned up. It seemed the hero-villain fight had done some serious damage to our school.

As we emerged from behind the Great Clock, we ran straight into Tabs, who hovered in the air with an envelope in her teeth. I plucked it from her. When she realized I didn't have any treat to offer her, she promptly bit my shoulder. Then she nuzzled and purred against Ileana's cheek and flew off.

"What's it say?" asked Wolf.

"My dad wants to see me in his study."

"Maybe he wants to thank you for saving him?" Ileana asked.

"Right," I said skeptically.

I said good-bye to my allies and made my way to the old man's office. As usual, it was crowded with old, musty books and jars crammed into cobwebby corners. His desk was littered with the familiar assortment of parchments. The skull still held a burning candle. The deathwatch beetle still ticked down the time to someone's death. And I was still left to stand even though a perfectly good chair was just inches away from me.

"Rune," my father said, looking up at last from his parchments.

"You could've told me," I said. He didn't have to ask what I meant.

"Well, you found out either way," he said stiffly.

"I mean, what if I'd wanted to date her? She's my sister! Eww!" I said.

"I would not have allowed it," he answered.

"How? You don't always know everything."

"Don't I?" he asked sharply. Then he stood and came around the desk to face me. I resisted the urge to back away. "I know that you stood up to Morgana. I know that you came to the hero school to rescue me. I know that you somehow stopped the attack on this school."

I smiled at his unexpected compliments.

"However," he continued. My smile faltered. "I also know you worked alongside one—what was his name, Tabs?" The cat-a-bat mewed at my father from her dusty corner. "Ah yes, *Invis-a-boy*. You made a serious mess of my corridors and nearly brought ruin on us all."

"But—but," I stammered. "I saved you! I saved the school! And you kept secrets from me! You never even told me Ileana was my sister, that the queen was my *mother*! And hey!" I said, just realizing something. "Does this mean I'm a prince?"

"I suppose it does," my father said.

"So shouldn't you bow to me or something?" I was joking, of course, but my dad didn't seem amused.

"Time to fulfill your royal duties, Prince Rune. You can start with cleaning up the mess your little hero friends left behind."

I remembered the scorch marks, the blasted cave walls, the melted and frozen and smashed chunks of debris that had fallen across the corridors like an avalanche.

My shoulders sagged as I left my dad's study. Outside, Ileana was waiting for me.

"How bad was it?" she asked.

"I have to clean the whole school," I said.

"Not so bad," she said.

"Not so—? Have you *looked* at this place?"

"Want some help?" The princess poked me playfully with her elbow.

"Yes!" I pleaded. "Wait, you're going to help me?"

"Of course!" said Ileana, already Spelling things back into place for me. "What are sisters for?"

Together, my sister and I worked the hours away until the school was back to normal. Exhausted, we walked back side by side until we reached the Great Clock. Then she hugged me.

"Hey, no hugging in the halls," I said, but I might have hugged her back. That's just a rumor, though. There were no witnesses.

ACKNOWLEDGMENTS

I was about eighty pages into this book when I realized the story had somehow gotten away from me, and I couldn't get it back. I was so frustrated. Then, one desperate night, I threw up my hands and said, "I have to start over!" My husband picked up a container I keep next to my computer labeled Random Plot Twists. In it are tiny pieces of paper with ideas from Internet plot generators. He pulled one at random and said, "Whatever this says, you're going to write about it." I laughed, filled with skeptical amusement, knowing nothing in that little box could really help me. Then my husband read the paper, and this is what it said: "There is a prophecy, and the villain is the one that's described as the hero."

You have just read the book I wrote based on that

little sentence. So, my first thanks goes to my husband, Ben, for his uncanny knack to draw the right piece of paper.

Of course, writing a book is just *one* part of the whole process. Someone has to have faith in it, has to edit it, has to make it all come together. Thanks to the following: Nancy Gallt Agency and Marietta Zacker for your faith and encouragement; all the amazing people at Bloomsbury, especially Caroline Abbey, who makes my writing look good; Kyra and Kaelyn, always my first audience; and Victor Rivas, whose artistic talent brings my characters to life. Thanks above all to the Author of Life, my inspiration each day.

And thank you, reader, for sharing in the adventure.

Stephanie S. Sanders grew up on an Iowa farm surrounded by fields, forests, and a little river. As a child, she believed these were magical places, harboring the secret worlds of fairies and unicorns. Stephanie is all grown up now, but she still lives in Iowa with her husband, Benjamin, and their two daughters, Kyra and Kaelyn, in a rickety old house. She has a cat named Pudge, a dog named Buddy, and a fish named Speedy Tomato. Stephanie enjoys reading and writing fantasy stories. Her other interests change daily but usually include: steampunk, Renaissance festivals, Celtic music, old houses, graveyards, photography, hiking, and all things chocolate. She is also the author of *Villain School: Good Curses Evil*.

www.stephsanders.com
www.villainkids.com